HOPPY HOLIDAY HOMICIDE

Pet Whisperer P.I.

MOLLY FITZ

Editor: Jennifer Lopez (No, seriously!)

Cover & Graphics Designer: Cover Affairs

Proofreader: Tabitha Kocsis & Alice Shepherd

Sweet Promise Press
PO Box 72
Brighton, MI 48116

ABOUT THIS BOOK

Nobody does the holidays like small-town Maine, and my particular small town just so happens to be the very best at decking the halls and rocking around the big Christmas tree downtown.

Yes, every year, Glendale puts on a Holiday Spectacular that's grander and greater than the one that came before. Unfortunately, the only thing everyone's going to remember this year is the two dead bodies that show up in the center of the ice sculpture garden.

With the whole town having come out to play, everyone's in close proximity to the crime scene—and everyone's a suspect. A great many fingers are pointed my way, too, since it was me and my cat that discovered the deathly duo. With only my whacky Nan, recently discovered cousin, overly optimistic Chihuahua, and snarky feline to help me, can I clear my name and save Christmas all in one perfectly executed investigation?

Hold on to your jingle bells, because it's going to be a wild ride.

AUTHOR'S NOTE

Hey, new reader friend!

Welcome to the crazy inner workings of my brain. I hope you'll find it a fun and exciting place to be.

If you love animals as much as I do, then I'm pretty sure you're going to enjoy the journey ahead.

Hoppy Holiday Homicide is just one of my many brain-tickling adventures! Many more will be coming soon, so make sure you sign up for my newsletter or download my app to help you stay in the know. Doing so also unlocks adorable pictures of my own personal feline overlords, Schrödinger and Merlin the Magical Fluff, deleted scenes from my books, bonus giveaways, and other cool things that are just for my inner circle of readers.

You can download my free app here:
mollymysteries.com/app

Or sign up for my newsletter here:
mollymysteries.com/subscribe

If you're ready to dive right into more Pet Whisperer P.I., then you can even order the next books right now by clicking below:

Retriever Ransom
Lawless Litter
Legal Seagull
Scheming Sphynx
Deer Duplicity
Persian Penalty
Grizzly Grievance

And make sure you've also read the books that come before **Hoppy Holiday Homicide** in the series. They can be read in any order, but you'll enjoy yourself more if you start at the beginning!

Okay, ready to talk to some animals and solve some mysteries?

Let's do this!
Molly Fitz

To anyone who wishes she could talk to her animal best friend…
Well, what's stopping you?

CHAPTER ONE

Hi. I'm Angie Russo, and while you may not immediately recognize it, I'm probably one of the most unusual people you'll ever meet.

Why?

Well, how many other people do you know who can communicate with animals? And, no, I'm not talking meows, woofs, and chirps. We have actual conversations, and we even solve crimes together—but I'm getting ahead of myself here.

Before I say any more—*shhh!*—my strange ability is a secret that must be protected at all costs. Not because I'm in danger or anything, just because I'd rather people not know.

Okay?

And, no, I'm not a witch, werewolf, or other kind of fictional supernatural creature. I'm just a normal girl in her late twenties who got electrocuted by an old coffee maker and woke up with the power to communicate with animals.

First, it was just the one cat, Octo-Cat as I call him. He was in the room when I got zapped. We were both there for a will reading, me as the lowly paralegal and him as the primary beneficiary.

When he realized I could understand him, he revealed that his late owner had been murdered even though everyone thought the rich old lady had died of natural causes. Turns out that wasn't what had happened at all.

She'd been murdered, and now he needed me to help him prove it.

Well, we got justice for Ethel Fulton and eventually wound up living in her stately manor home. Since none of the relatives wanted Octo-Cat and I really, really wanted him, we ended up together, too.

We live with my eccentric grandmother,

who's known around these parts simply as Nan. A few months ago, we also adopted a rescue Chihuahua named Paisley. She's the sugar to Octo-Cat's spice, and the cute little thing can never say a bad word about anyone...

Well, except the naughty raccoon named Pringle who lives in our backyard. He used to live under the porch, but then he kind of blackmailed us into building him a custom treehouse—two treehouses, actually. Oh, boy, is that a long story.

Speaking of long stories, I've got several of those. Just you wait.

You see, a lot has changed in the months since Octo-Cat and I officially opened our P.I. business together. We haven't had a single paying client yet, but we're still getting tons of experience by accidentally stumbling into one mystery after the next.

Hey, whatever works. Right?

Oh, also, I'm in love with my boyfriend and former boss, Charles Longfellow, III— although I haven't exactly told him that yet. Octo-Cat is also in a long-distance relation-ship with a former show cat and minor Instagram influencer named Grizabella. And he never stops telling her—or anyone who will listen—just how much he loves her. He's even started giving me guff about how slow Charles and I are moving by comparison.

Then there's the fact that we've discovered Nan isn't actually biologically related to me or my mom, but we're still working on digging up the full story there. Yes, this entire time, she hasn't understood the reason we were shoved together, either.

On the positive side of that crazy bit of news, we have connected with long-lost family in Larkhaven, Georgia. I was supposed to visit them last month, but a murder derailed our travel plans just a bit. So, instead, my cousin Mags showed up here and is staying through the end of the month.

Mags is a hoot, and we all love her. She and I have so much in common and look so much alike that I sometimes wonder if we're not actually twins instead of just cousins.

She's a couple years older than me, though, and as far as I can tell, she's completely normal. Her family owns a candle shop in her town's historic district, and she's promised to teach Nan and me how to make our own candles before she heads back home.

We have lots to do before that happens, though.

For one thing, it's almost Christmas. Nan keeps all of us busy with the custom advent calendar she made at one of her community art classes, and today we're also scheduled to head into town for the twelfth annual Holiday Spectacular!

The Holiday Spectacular is a time-honored tradition for our small town of Glendale. People come from all over Blueberry Bay to gather around the big tree downtown, compete in the ice sculpture competition, and celebrate Christmas with the staggering variety of small businesses downtown.

We get everything from hot cocoa stations to learning Christmas carols from around the world to meeting local authors and getting signed books from them to...

Well, each year is completely different, and that's what makes it so much fun. I can't wait to show Mags my hometown at its best. I hope she'll love it every bit as much as I do.

Hey, look at that, it's time to go find out!

I smacked my lips together after dragging my new cranberry red lip stain across them. Perfect for the holidays. Normally, I wore very little makeup, since my clothes made enough of a statement without any outside help. Lately, though, Nan had begun insisting I put a little more effort into my appearance. She claimed it was for all the holiday festivities, but I suspected she secretly hoped that my glamorous new efforts might rub off on my cousin, Mags.

It's not that Mags was plain, but she did prefer a simple, non-fussy wardrobe. While working in her family's candle shop in the historic district, she sometimes wore old-fashioned clothing with big skirts and a bonnet— and I suspected that was all the fuss she could handle. I didn't blame her for wanting to keep it easy during her leisure time.

Mags's signature knock sounded at my bedroom door—three short, one long, two short again.

"Come in!" I called, turning away from the mirror and toward the door.

Mags wore a white button-down shirt and white skirt with white flats. Her white-blonde hair fell midway down her waist, and her fair skin had not a stitch of makeup on it. She looked like a snow angel... or a ghost.

"Can I borrow an outfit from you today?" she asked with a frown. "I think I'm letting Nan down with my color choices."

I laughed. "Don't worry about Nan. I let her down constantly. She still loves us both, though."

"She offered to let me wear something from her wardrobe, but Angie—" Mags dropped her voice to a whisper and motioned for me to lean closer. "Everything's hot pink!"

We broke apart in giggles.

"Seriously, though, please help a cousin out," she begged, joining her hands in front of her and shaking them at me.

I skipped toward the closet, loving every minute of having my long-lost cousin here. I couldn't believe we had little more than a week left together. I was going to miss her so much when she went back home.

"How's this?" I asked, tossing a Santa-print party dress at her. It was the same one

I'd worn when we took the pets to get their pictures done with Santa at the pet shop in Dewdrop Springs. While it was one of my favorites, I had tons of holiday wear that hadn't made it out of the closet yet this year.

That was the thing about doing most of my shopping at Goodwill: everything was so cheap and went toward a good cause, so I had zero issue indulging my addiction. Today I wore a pair of jeans with the ugliest Christmas sweater I owned—it had giant pom-poms stuck in a huge ring to form a three-dimensional Christmas wreath, complete with jingle bells and a giant satin ribbon.

It was wretched, and I adored it.

"This is perfect," Mags said after a quick appraisal of the dress.

"Goes good with pigtails," I said.

She turned crimson. "I think that's perhaps a little too much for today."

Octo-Cat trotted in with Paisley following close behind.

"Mommy, you look gorgeous!" the Chihuahua cried.

"One day that sweater will be mine," my

tabby swore. "You can't tell me that's not meant to be a cat toy. Look at all those mischievous floofs!"

Well, he had me there.

"Mommy, can I come, too?" Paisley asked, her tail wagging so fast that it was little more than a black blur.

"She can't talk to us in front of Mags, genius," Octo-Cat said, looking bored with the whole thing.

Mags smiled at me, probably wondering why I had suddenly stopped talking when the animals entered. Let's just say it was incredibly hard to keep my secret from her, especially considering she was family. Still, the fewer people who knew, the better. And I didn't know if she would even believe me. I didn't want to send her screaming back to Georgia and ruin our relationship with the rest of the family before we even got the chance to meet them.

Just one more week to go. I could keep my secret for that long...

Um, right?

CHAPTER TWO

Mags looked absolutely adorable wearing my Santa-print dress. She complemented the look with a fuzzy white beret and then asked for my help applying that new cranberry stain to her lips and a bit of blush to her cheeks.

"Selfie time!" she cried, maneuvering her phone to capture a photo of us from several angles.

"Wow, we really do look alike," I said when she showed me the resulting pictures. Despite her fairer coloring, we both had the same brown eyes, perky nose, and heart-shaped face. She had the perfect poise of a supermodel while I had somehow managed to give myself a triple chin and the viewer a front-row view straight up my nostrils.

This right here was why I didn't find myself addicted to social media the way so many others in my age bracket tended to be. I'd much rather be behind the camera than in front of it, but if given the choice, I'd go for no cameras at all. I could thank being raised by two newscasters for that.

"You're way more photogenic than me," I mumbled as Mags texted our selfie to a few family members back in Georgia. I hadn't met any of them yet and wasn't super thrilled with the awful photo being one of their first introductions to me.

"It comes with lots and lots of practice," Mags revealed with a coy smile. Unlike me, she seemed much more comfortable interacting with people online as opposed to in person. "I'm on screen a lot for my candle-making videos, so I've learned my angles."

"Girls!" Nan called from the bottom of the stairs that led to my bedroom tower. "Ready to paint the town red? And green?" She chuckled at her own joke as she moved down the grand staircase and into the foyer.

Mags looked to me for confirmation as she stuck her phone into her small handbag and pulled at the hem on her borrowed dress.

A huge smile crossed my face as I yelled, "Coming!"

Mags, the animals, and I pounded down the two flights of stairs to the foyer where Nan had relocated to bundle up in an eclectic assortment of bright pink winter wear.

Nan pulled out a tiny brown jacket and knelt on the floor. "Paisley, come here, you sweet dog!"

The Chihuahua ran, her whole back half wiggling with joy. "Yes, Nan. Coming, Nan. I love you, Nan."

While she called me "Mommy," her greatest loyalty definitely lay with Nan. I'd asked her about that once, and she said that she couldn't remember what it felt like to have a mother since she'd lost hers when she was still too young to remember. Since Nan insisted on being called *Nan* by everyone who knew her—and because she couldn't communicate with Paisley the way I could—the little dog had taken to referring to me as *Mommy*.

She stood mostly still now as Nan worked

her legs and head through the little brown jacket, which upon closer inspection was actually a reindeer costume. The hood had two tall, erect antlers that put Paisley off balance somewhat as she hopped away from Nan and attempted to prance about the house.

"Mags, you look lovely," Nan said as she straightened back into a standing position. "And you're well-matched to Paisley in that Santa dress, which is good because I'll need you to keep an eye on her while we're out."

"Oh, are you not coming?"

Nan shrugged into her hot pink coat lined with black faux fur around the collar and cuffs. "Of course I'm coming. But I need both arms for hugging all my old friends who only journey home for the holidays. Paisley will have a much better time with you."

I stepped forward and grabbed Octo-Cat's neon green leash and harness from the back of our coat closet. He hated having to wear it, especially since he'd gotten better about being off leash during our outdoor adventures. Unfortunately for him, I'd be with Mags the whole time today, which meant

I couldn't use our ability to converse to keep him in line.

At the end of the day, safety won every time, which meant the harness was non-negotiable. Of course, that didn't stop my cat from trying.

"I'm not wearing that," he said, glaring at me as he spoke. "Last time you put it on me, Santa Claus got murdered. And before that, you granted me a favor in exchange for my compliance. That was a long time ago, so as far as I'm concerned, you owe me a whole new favor if you expect me to wear that thing today."

I shook my head and bit my tongue to keep from talking. The favor he'd tricked me into granting was the purchase of this giant manor home, since he didn't like my previous rental. As much as I liked the luxe estate now, I didn't think him wearing the harness a handful of times over the past year and a half was anywhere near equivalent of an ask.

I reached for Octo-Cat with both hands and he swatted at me.

"No, Angela. No!"

"I don't think he wants to wear that,"

Mags said with a nervous laugh. "Why are we bringing him, anyway? It seems to me that an outdoor festival wouldn't be very fun for a cat."

"Trust me, I'll never hear the end of it if I leave him behind," I said, then quickly added, "He'll be yowling for days to punish me, and mostly at night, because he's got an evil streak a mile wide."

"Smart cat."

"You have no idea." I chuckled with relief. You'd think I'd be better at minding my secret after so much time, but you'd be very, very wrong.

"Well, here." Mags grabbed Octo-Cat so quickly neither he nor I saw it coming. "Let me help."

He struggled and spun in her arms, but Mags held on tight while I worked the harness onto his furry little body. "You will live to regret this, Angela, and it might not be all that long."

I set him on the ground and stifled a laugh as he took a couple steps, twitched, and then frantically began to lick his fur where it touched the neon green straps.

"Are we all ready to go?" Nan asked cheerfully, completely unbothered by the angry kitty standing near her feet. While Octo-Cat generally held me to a higher standard of behavior and let Nan's foibles pass by unmentioned, one of these days, he'd get her, and he'd get her good. Hopefully, he'd at least wait until after the holidays.

A minute later we'd all piled into my sedan, and less than fifteen minutes later we'd arrived downtown for Glendale's Holiday Spectacular.

Even though it was early, we had to park several blocks away in order to get a spot.

"Wow," Mags said when downtown finally came into view. "It's like we're inside a snow globe."

We had half a foot of snow at best, but Mags never got white Christmases at home in Georgia, so I let her enjoy the moment without explaining the snowfall was actually light for this time of year.

"Welcome! Welcome to the Holiday Spectacular!" Mr. Gable, the owner of our only local jewelry store and the head of the planning committee, greeted us with his pet rabbit in one hand and an old-fashioned camera in the other. He wore a Santa costume without the classic fur-trimmed coat, revealing black suspenders on top of his thick wooly undershirt. "Have a seat on the sleigh. Let Santa and E.B. take your picture."

"E.B.?" Mags asked as she and I slid into the rear seat of the sleigh and Nan jumped up front with both animals.

"It's short for Easter Bunny," I explained, having just met the bunny for the first time myself earlier that month when we went to the pet store for photos with Santa and ended up solving a murder mystery instead. "Apparently, she was an Easter gift for the grandkids gone wrong. He was quick to rescue the bunny and give her a better life, and the two have been together ever since."

Mr. Gable set E.B. in the nearby nativity scene which had been lined with hay and outfitted with food and water for the little rabbit, then he stepped forward to take our picture.

"Do you see that?" Octo-Cat demanded just as Mr. Gable instructed us all to say cheese. "That ridiculous rabbit has the exact

same harness as me. I've never been so humil-
iated in all my life. Oh, you will pay mightily
for this, dear Angela."

Sure enough, E.B. also wore a neon green
harness, although she didn't seem to mind
nearly as much as Octo-Cat did. In fact, she'd
already fallen asleep cuddled up sweetly in
baby Jesus's manger.

CHAPTER THREE

After getting our photo snapped at Santa's sleigh, we made our way over to the extreme cocoa station. Here, festival-goers could order crazy custom concoctions with more flavor and mix-in varieties than even made sense for a cup of hot chocolate.

Seeing as we'd arrived at the very start of the festival, the crowds were still sparse, and that came with the added bonus of no lines. Mags and I stepped right up to the outdoor counter and ordered the unicorn drink made with white chocolate and swirled with raspberry, rainbow marshmallows, pink drizzle, sprinkles, and a gold-and-white candy cane horn. We watched in awe as the barista whipped up our order.

Nan took this opportunity to shout a quick goodbye and then disappear on the arm of a comely silver-haired gentleman I don't think I recognized. Nan knew everyone both in town and outside of it, but she hadn't dated a single soul since my grandpa's death more than a decade earlier. Judging by her coquettish laughter and sparkling eyes, I'd definitely have to learn more about this mysterious new friend of hers.

For now, however, I'd simply focus on this special time spent with my cousin and our two favorite animal companions as downtown Glendale did what it does best—celebrate the season.

"There you are," my mother crooned, rushing over to saddle both me and Mags with giant warm hugs. "Merry Christmas! Happy Holiday Spectacular!"

"Merry Christmas Eve, Mom," I said, grabbing my freshly delivered unicorn cocoa from the pop-up table and dropping a tip in the barista's gift-wrapped jar. It felt a bit odd to be wishing her a happy eve when it was hardly even ten o'clock in the morning.

The Spectacular ran from ten in the morning to ten at night, giving people all day to drop by and enjoy the festivities. Most favored the night hours because of the majesty and wonder added by the light displays, but I knew the committee was working hard under Mr. Gable to get more folks coming out early and spreading a steady stream of business out over the entire day.

"Where's Dad?" I asked, then took that first decadent sip of my sugary drink. *Mmm.*

Mom studied her reflection using her camera's selfie mode and fluffed up her hair as she answered. "The first reindeer game is about to begin, so naturally he's covering it for the station. It's the three-hooved race, sure to be a lot of fun."

Dad did the sports report for the local news while Mom was an anchor. She covered a lot of human-interest pieces around Maine, especially now that their broadcasts were viewed regionally, thanks to her role in solving the beloved Senator Harlow's murder.

And, naturally, the Holiday Spectacular had been big news since it first started. Tourists now came from out of state to celebrate the season with us, and each year, the festival became bigger and bigger, thanks in part to Mom's ace coverage of the event and to the expert leadership under Mr. Gable.

"I need to get back," Mom said, glancing back over her shoulder toward the games field. "But I saw the two of you from across the way and figured I'd dash over to ask a quick favor."

"We'd be happy to help," Mags said as she held Paisley tucked under one arm and the steaming souvenir mug filled with cocoa in her other hand. "Just tell us how."

"Great. It shouldn't take too much of your time, but it is really important. I'm afraid the judges for the ice sculpture competition are no-shows. Would the two of you mind filling in?"

"Not at all," Mags said, shaking her head so hard, some of her cocoa splashed onto the freshly shoveled street below. "Oops! Sorry about that. It sounds like a lot of fun judging, though. I'd be happy to help, if Angie is up for it."

"Wonderful. We have over thirty entries, if you can believe that, but you don't need to write up score cards or anything. Just pick first, second, and third place, and text me with what you decide. The ice sculpture garden is at the far end of our setup near the bridge and the little park. Think you can find it?"

"I know we can," I answered, taking a step toward Mom but being unable to go any farther without yanking my stubborn cat who refused to move from the spot. "Now go get back to Dad before you miss out on that race."

"Will do," Mom said, already jogging back in the direction from which she'd come. "Thanks again, girls."

"What do you say? Should we go now?" Mags asked, then took that first tentative sip from her half-emptied unicorn cocoa. Her eyes grew wide and her head shot back. "Wow, that's a lot of sugar."

I took another swig of mine and moaned

in pleasure. "If you ask me, it's exactly right. Then again, you probably don't eat Nan's homemade baked goods every day of the week."

"I wish I did, though!" Mags enthused as we wound our way through the fancifully adorned streets.

We strolled past a number of local craftsmen and women peddling their wares, and I spied a particularly eye-catching necklace that I wanted to make sure we came back for once our judging duties were behind us.

Mags stopped dead in her tracks and gasped with glee. "Whoa, are those live reindeer?"

I laughed at the look of wonder that overtook my cousin. I'd been coming to the Holiday Spectacular since it was first founded twelve years ago, but I was sure seeing it all for the first time would make anyone drop her jaw to her chest like Mags was now.

"Yup, eight of them. There are also sheep, goats, pigs, and even a camel. It's a full petting zoo. Part Santa's workshop and part little town of Bethlehem."

"We've gotta come back." Mags grabbed my hands and gave one last longing look toward the animals. "I'm petting every single thing they've got in there."

"I promise we will," I said, squeezing both of her hands then letting go.

"I'd rather not spend my precious time around stinky, sweating cattle," Octo-Cat groused.

Well, too bad for him. He'd complain about whatever we did, and Mags was truly excited to come back and spend time among the reindeer.

We strode past more pop-up restaurants, merchants, and local groups manning their booths, progressing nearly a full block in our trek before Mags ground to a halt once again. "Candles!" she cried. "Oh my heart!"

I nodded toward the pair of women sitting outside the tent. Mags had already disappeared inside where it was dark, save for the glow of tealight candles set up carefully around the inside.

"She makes candles for a living," I explained to the ladies sitting outside the tent.

I felt odd standing here with them while Mags was inside but knew better than to take my cat and dog into a space with open flames. "Yours are beautiful. How much are they?"

"We're not selling the candles," the younger of the two women explained with a kind smile. "We make and sell menorahs. Other members of our synagogue are also set up selling potato latkes a few booths down."

"Oh, for Hanukkah. I've never celebrated myself but have always loved the story about the Maccabees and the miracle of the oil."

"It's not just a story," the older woman said. "It's God working miracles. He still does that to this day, you know."

"How much is this?" Mags asked, rejoining us with a small silver menorah in her hands.

The women told her the amount, and she handed over a couple twenties. "Thank you. I will cherish it always. Happy Hanukkah."

"Happy Hanukkah," the women called after us as we continued toward the ice sculpture garden.

"They have a bit of everything here. Don't they?" Mags asked.

"You have no idea," I said with a giggle. "Just wait until we check out some of the reindeer games."

"I'm glad we got here nice and early. There's so much to do, I'm afraid we won't have time for it all."

"Well, here's the ice sculpture garden. Let's make sure we give each contestant fair consideration, then pick our winners and get back to the streets."

We crossed the road and entered the park where rows of enormous and intricately carved ice statues stood in a spiral configuration. A sign at the beginning of the path read: "Start here and follow the path until you reach the center. Once there, follow the red ribbon for a shortcut back to the start. Enjoy!"

"It's like the Guggenheim," I said, thinking of the fantastic museum I'd studied during my humanities coursework. "You never have to turn or think about where to go next, freeing you up to enjoy art for art's sake."

"Look at this one!" Mags cried, already a few sculptures down the path and admiring the carving of a swan splashing into water with wings spread wide. "Isn't it lovely?"

"How about this one?" I said pointing to a giant, elaborate snowflake. "It must have taken so much time to get all the details exactly right."

"It's sad that this gorgeous art is all going to melt away." Mags stood in front of the statue of a woman wearing a gorgeous flowing gown now. "And it's going to be very hard to pick just three to win."

"Let's start by just looking. Then when we reach the center, instead of taking the shortcut out, we can walk through again and try to make a short list of our favorites."

Mags nodded. "So far, everything is my favorite."

"It may take a few back and forths," I agreed. "So let's get started."

We walked through the spiral, admiring sculptures of animals, people, nature, and even abstract creations. Hardly any time had passed at all before we wound up in the center, and a swatch of bright red caught the corner of my eye. I turned toward it, expecting to see the promised ribbon that would guide festivalgoers out of the garden and prevent traffic jams.

Instead I saw deep pools of crimson marring the otherwise pristine snow. *Blood.*

CHAPTER FOUR

My eyes darted to Mags, who stood trembling like a leaf in the wind.

"Is that b-b-blood?" she stammered, allowing Paisley to leap from her arms to the ground below. I hated it when the small dog took these bold leaps, but somehow she never seemed to get hurt when she collided with the ground.

Octo-Cat yanked on his leash. "Of course it's blood, genius. What else would it be?"

I glowered at him, sorely wishing I could reprimand him for being so insensitive in this delicate situation. "Yes," I whispered carefully to Mags. "And where there's blood, there may be a body. At least that's been my experience. Wait here while I take a look around."

Mags trembled even more violently and refused to meet my eyes. She kept her gaze fixed on the deep red as it crept through the snow, feeling more dangerous with each new inch it gained. Her hands shook harder and harder, sloshing the remaining cocoa from her mug.

Wow. Maybe Mags and I weren't quite as similar as I had once thought. While I didn't exactly enjoy finding myself in these situations, I'd learned to mostly control my emotions so that I could focus on the mystery rather than the horror. Mags, on the other hand, had already become a terrified, blubbering wreck—as most normal people would, I supposed.

I ran forward and took the cup from her, then set it on the ground with mine. Both of us had most definitely lost our appetite for the sweet stuff, anyway.

Paisley nuzzled my leg with her snout. "Mommy, is there a bad guy nearby? Is he going to hurt us?"

Without thinking, I scooped the little dog up, placing her under one arm, and grabbed Octo-Cat with my other.

"Angela, unhand me. I am not your cuddle toy. That's what this one's for," he said, jerking his head toward Paisley.

I remained quiet as we crept between the ice sculptures, searching for the source of the blood. It didn't take long for me to spot a large hand lying palm up beside a sculpture of a Christmas tree. I swallowed hard and stepped in for a closer look. There I found not one but two fresh corpses—one facing the sky with unseeing eyes and the other face down in the cold snow. From above, a light sprinkling of snowflakes danced through the air and landed on the bodies, giving them an impromptu beginning to their burials.

"Are these the missing judges?" I whispered.

"That would be the obvious conclusion," my tabby said, squirming beneath my arm.

My own blood ran cold as I wondered why someone would resort to murder and whether Mags and I were now at risk, having been the ones to take their places.

That's when I saw a thick glistening spear of ice rising from the smaller corpse's back. She'd been impaled by an icicle, and it was already beginning to melt. Fat water droplets ran down the spear and drenched her already blood-soaked jacket.

I turned back toward the man expecting to find a similar weapon emerging from his chest, but there was no murder weapon to be found. I briefly searched for any signs of strangulation, stabbing, gunshot wounds, or any other method of murder I'd come across in my year and a half as an investigator.

Nothing.

Paisley, dressed in her elaborate reindeer costume, leapt from my arms and crept over to the victims and licked at their cheeks. "Mommy, Mommy, are they going to be okay? Will they wake up soon?" This made me realize that Paisley hadn't seen nearly as many dead bodies as Octo-Cat and I had in our day. Poor thing was probably every bit as terrified as Mags.

Octo-Cat curled his upper lip, content now to remain in my arms. "Surely even you can't be that dense, dog." He loved his

33

Chihuahua sister and only took to calling her *dog* when he was feeling particularly superior, which, I guess, was still quite a lot of the time.

"Quiet," I muttered almost absent-mindedly. "Let me think."

"A-A-A-Angie," Mags stuttered, her voice rising above the tall sculptures and crashing back down on me. "What's going on? Is everything okay?" From the tone of her voice, she clearly already knew the answer. Still, I'd need to tell her what I'd found, then we'd have to tell the authorities together.

With one last lingering glance toward the poor people who had come to enjoy the Holiday Spectacular but had ended up as dead as grandma after she got ran over by the reindeer, I took a deep centering breath and returned to my cousin. "We need to find Officer Bouchard and let him know there's been a murder."

Mags cried out as if in physical pain. "Really? A murder? Here? But, but... everyone seems so nice."

I frowned as I tried to remember a time when I had been so innocently optimistic.

Never, I thought. I'd always been too bookish not to be at least somewhat suspicious of the world around me. I used to consider myself paranoid, but that was before bodies started piling up whenever I was near.

Mags stared at me with wide eyes as she waited for an answer that wouldn't come. She wanted me to take it back, to make everything okay again, but I simply couldn't.

Instead, I nodded. "Yes, unfortunately. Actually, there's been two. And we have to get the police. Now."

I dropped Octo-Cat into the snow and grabbed Mags by the hand, yanking her along as I wound my way back through the spiral garden.

Octo-Cat followed behind on his leash, yelling the most profane kitty curses that had ever spilled off his sandpaper tongue. He could be angry for all I cared. Some things were more important than following the many elaborate and contradictory rules he'd established to govern our lives.

Besides, unlike Paisley, he always landed on his feet.

I wasn't quite so sure Mags and I would be as lucky, especially when a dark figure swept across the quiet garden moving quickly and coming straight for us.

CHAPTER FIVE

The dark figure drew closer, but still not close enough for me to make out his features or intent.

Mags yanked out of my hold and stopped cold, seemingly unsure of whether to run, hide, or do some strange combination of both. Instead of doing either, she stood a couple paces before me, frozen like a shocked deer on a lonely country road.

I braced myself for the worst and turned around to get a good look at the new arrival. His silver badge flashed brilliantly in the sunlight, set against a dark blue uniform shirt. He continued to close the distance between us quickly, concern pinching at his features. *Not a threat. Not a threat at all.*

"Officer Bouchard," I cried, elated that he had found us and realizing that maybe I was still a bit paranoid, after all.

Mags visibly relaxed and took a tentative step toward us.

"I heard screams," he said, moving his hand to the gun at his hip. "Is everything okay here?"

Mags's face reddened as she tried to push an entire dictionary's worth of words from her mouth at once. "Oh, it's horrible. There's blood. Lots of blood. Angie saw bodies. She said there's two. People died. And I don't know who they were or who killed them. But it's so scary. Things like this never happen back home in Larkhaven. Aunt Linda says trouble won't find you unless you go looking for it yourself. But I swear, we just wanted to enjoy the festival. And now Angie is acting like it's up to us to figure out what happened here. I don't know who the victims are. I don't know who the killer is. I don't know anything other than I think I need to go home." Finally finished, her voice cracked, and Mags drew back into herself.

Officer Bouchard stayed on high alert. "Whoa there, slow down. Start by telling me who you are and how you discovered the bodies."

I placed a hand on Mags's shoulder to let her know that I could handle things from here. "Go get some latkes or more cocoa or gingerbread cookies, or something. I'll catch Officer Bouchard up on what we discovered."

"Should I go with her, Mommy?" Paisley asked from somewhere near my ankle.

"Mags," I called after her. "Take Paisley with you."

The little dog took off running and also barking, though for no apparent reason.

I watched until Mags scooped her into a cuddle, then I turned back to the waiting policeman. "Let me show you what we found."

As we walked the short distance to the hulking Christmas tree sculpture and the bodies that lay behind it, I informed Officer Bouchard of the no-show judges and the last-minute change up that required Mags and me to take their places. I also explained that Mags was my cousin visiting from Georgia.

"I didn't know you had family in Georgia," he said, tilting his head to study me as we walked.

"Neither did we. At least not until a couple months ago. Anyway, here's the crime scene." I motioned toward the bodies, even though he couldn't have missed them if he'd been blind in one eye and couldn't see out the other.

"Are we done now?" Octo-Cat groused. "I know your imagination's already running wild with a hundred thousand ideas of who done it and why. But I heard that the Little Dog Diner has a booth set up somewhere around here, and Octavius needs himself a lobster roll."

It took all the strength not to roll my eyes at this expression of my cat's misplaced priorities. Thankfully, I think I managed to pull it off. Studying the melting ice weapon, I asked the officer, "Do you know who they are?"

Officer Bouchard hooked his thumbs

through his beltloops and rocked on his heels. "Can't see the woman's face, but the man I recognize as Fred Hapley. He sells health insurance all across the state, and I'm pretty sure he's one of the missing judges you mentioned. If memory serves, he was also a last-minute addition."

My breaths rose in icy little puffs as I thought about where we should take things from here. "My mom should be able to confirm it and let us know who the other judge was supposed to be and whether this is her. She's not technically on the planning committee, but she'll have memorized the setup before coming out as part of planning her news piece. Should I call her over?"

Officer Bouchard sucked air through his teeth. "Not just yet, if you don't mind. Your mother's a good woman and an ace reporter, but I need some time to investigate and call in backup before the press gets involved. You understand, don't you?"

I nodded vigorously. No one understood my mother's drive to get the story at any cost better than I did. "What are you going to do when festivalgoers start coming through the sculpture garden?" I asked, worried we'd end up creating a scene whether or not we wanted one.

He quirked one eyebrow. "You said you and your cousin are the new judges, right?"

"Yep."

"Then why don't you get her back here? And you two can guard the entrance so that nobody wanders inside."

"There's an exit, too," I pointed out, searching for that red ribbon the sign had mentioned.

"Well, that's perfect then," he said with a grin. "There are two ways in, and there are two of you. I shouldn't need long, but I sure do appreciate your help in keeping this under wraps."

"Okay, let me go find Mags," I said, hating to leave before we'd figured out much of anything.

"Finally," Octo-Cat grumbled. "I'm starving. I may have even lost a life because of it. I can't believe you've made me wait so long for my lobster roll."

Little did he know his lobster roll was not even close to next on our agenda. I had to find Mags, and then I had to find out what had happened to the slain judge and the as-of-yet unidentified body.

CHAPTER SIX

I found Mags at the latke stall, pushing potato pancakes dipped in applesauce into her mouth almost faster than she could chew them.

"Oh, I didn't know you'd be coming back so soon," she mumbled with one hand covering her mouth politely. "Otherwise, I would have saved you some." Her face turned red with embarrassment. "I'm a nervous eater, you see. These things didn't stand a chance."

I laughed and shook my head, happy to see her at least a little more relaxed than she'd been a few minutes back. "No judgment here.

We have to get back to help Officer
Bouchard, anyway."

Mags tossed her trash into a nearby canister
and wiped her mouth with the side of her hand.
"Are you sure we have to go back there? I don't
know if this kind of thing happens often here,
but I'm not used to dead bodies turning up back
home in Georgia." She said this with more of a
Southern twang than usual, no doubt longing
for the safety of good ol' reliable Larkhaven.

"Well, it's kind of my job as a P.I.," I
explained with a shrug. "Although it's not
always murder. Sometimes I deal with other
kinds of crooks, too."

"But can't we just enjoy the Holiday
Spectacular? You've told me so much about
it, and I've been looking forward to this part
of our visit. Plus, you might not be scared
that there's a murderer on the loose, but I
sure am. Maybe we can make a quick circuit
and then get the heck out of here."

I looped my arm through my cousin's and
marched back with her toward the ice sculpture garden. "We just need to do this one
quick thing to help out Officer Bouchard, and

then we'll get back to the festivities, I promise."

"Where's my lobster roll?" Octo-Cat whined, then growled, then sighed in defeat. "Unhook me from this hideous torture device, and I'll go grab one for myself, seeing as you're proving to be rather useless today."

Paisley growled from deep within her throat. "Don't talk to Mommy that way. She's busy being a superhero, and it's our job to be her sidekicks."

Octo-Cat tensed on the end of his leash. He definitely thought of himself as the Sherlock to my Watson, so Paisley's suggestion that I was the one in charge was sure to rankle.

"In case you haven't noticed," he said with a sneer, "she's pretending we're not even here. So, why do we owe her anything when there's really no way to help?"

Now it was Paisley who whined as her prick ears fell back against her neck while her tail went between her legs. "Just because it's not easy doesn't mean it's not the right thing to do."

"Oh, dear sweet dogling, you have so

much to learn. For starters, the best life should always be easy and also filled with sunspots and Evian and my long-overdue lobster roll."

Hard as it was to not jump into that particular conversation, I kept my eyes glued straight ahead and my feet focused on returning to the crime scene as quickly as possible.

Mags seemed to wilt more and more the closer we drew to the garden.

"Sorry for dragging you into this," I offered with an apologetic smile. "But it will be over soon. He just needs the area secured until backup can arrive."

We reached the sculpture of a crystalline rose that marked the start of the spiral viewing trail. I left Mags there and headed toward the exit.

"Wait! Where are you going?" she called after me, trembling uncertainty returning to her voice.

"I'll just be over there, keeping an eye on the exit. If you take a few steps out onto the street, you'll even be able to see me," I explained calmly. "Text if you need anything, even if it's just to chat and pass the time. We'll be finished up here before you know it, and then we can let the police handle the rest. Okay?"

Mags nodded, but a row of worry lines stretched across her normally smooth forehead. "Great. But now that I've had time to think about it, I'd really rather just find Nan and go home as soon as we're able. I don't feel so safe anymore."

As much as I loved the Holiday Spectacular, I loved my cousin so much more and wanted her to leave Blueberry Bay with happy memories instead of horrible ones. I'd do whatever it took to salvage our holiday.

"That's okay," I said with what I hoped was a reassuring smile. "We'll make our own fun. How do fresh-baked cookies and a Hallmark Channel Christmas movie sound for tonight?"

Mags smiled bravely and bobbed her head. "Sounds like a plan, Ms. Pet Whisperer P.I."

I chuckled as I walked away to take my place at the garden exit. First, though, I dipped into the center to let Officer Bouchard know Mags and I were on duty. Once I'd returned to the end of that red ribbon trail, I pulled out my phone and opened a group text with my mom and dad.

There's been a murder in the ice sculpture garden.

Officer Bouchard is securing the scene while Mags and I make sure no one wanders in.

After that, we're going to head home.

Mags is feeling a bit scared by everything.

Can you guys see that Nan gets home okay?

I asked in a series of fast texts.

Both my parents texted back immediately.

"Are you serious?" Mom's read.

"Are you safe?" Dad asked.

"I'm fine," I replied, "but I also don't think we'll be able to finish our judging duties before heading home."

"Poor Mags," Mom lamented with a frowny face emoji. "This is not the best introduction to our quiet corner of the world."

Although I didn't say it, I actually thought it was the perfect way to show my new cousin how life had been for us lately. Ever since I first met that snarky talking tabby a year and half ago, my entire life had been one danger, one investigation after the next.

Thanks to us, crime didn't pay around these parts, but apparently it also didn't rest. Not even for the holidays.

An incoming call lit up my screen. This one was from Nan. "What's this I hear about you and Mags leaving early?" she demanded, though her voice remained cheerful.

"Well, the murders kind of cramp the style of our Holiday Spectacular," I explained in a whisper, making sure none of the people further down the block heard.

"Well, that's really too bad. Could you do me a quick favor and ask Mags if I can get her anything from the artist's corner? I'm sure she'd at least like a souvenir or two. Right?"

I heard a deep voice speaking faintly on the other end but couldn't make out the words. "Who's there with you, Nan?"

"Just my friend, Mr. Milton," she answered dismissively. "Now, can you ask Mags about those souvenirs for me, please?"

"Sure, I'll check with her in a little bit. Right now, we're guarding the crime scene, and there are two different entrances. It's not a very good time to—"

"You're at the ice sculpture garden. Aren't

you? That place isn't very big. Just run over and ask her so that I know."

I sighed but still followed her instructions. There was little point in arguing with Nan when she wanted something—especially something quick and relatively easy like this.

Clutching my phone tightly in one hand and Octo-Cat beneath my other arm, I power walked over to the front entrance of the garden with Paisley following close at my heels. I was just rounding the corner when I caught sight of Mags.

Her eyes were wide, and her fair features looked even paler than usual as a hooded figure dragged her into the back of a cargo van, slammed the door, and sped away...

CHAPTER SEVEN

I dropped everything I'd been holding into the fresh snowbank at the side of the road and took off running after the van.

"Even though I land on my feet, it still hurts to be dropped, you know," Octo-Cat shouted after me.

But I had no time to respond. I put everything I had into following that van even though I knew I'd never be able to catch it on foot. Perhaps I would still be able to make out the license plate or catch a glimpse of the driver, something, anything to keep me connected with Mags.

I squinted hard at the departing vehicle, trying so hard. I didn't wear glasses, but I'd always been a bit nearsighted due to my obsession with reading. And unfortunately for Mags now, I couldn't make out a single digit beneath the dried mud that coated the plate.

I stopped running and bent over with my hands on my knees, gasping for breath while Paisley continued to run and bark up a storm drawing the curious stares of all who were near.

"Get back here, you bad guy!" the Chihuahua shouted. "It's not nice to take people when they don't want to be taken. Bad human, bad, bad."

Once I caught my breath a little, I scanned the downtown area for Octo-Cat but came up short. Maybe he'd gone to get that lobster roll after all, or maybe he was off somewhere nursing his wounded pride—both at having been dropped so unceremoniously into the snow and at having been forced to wear the harness he so loathed.

A burst of bright pink flashed onto the scene. Nan had arrived, and unlike me, she didn't appear winded in the slightest.

"You dropped this," she said, pushing my

fallen phone into my hand. "And you worried me silly. What happened?"

I couldn't help the tears that splashed onto my cheeks. It was one thing to find the bodies of people I'd never know and quite another to witness my cousin's kidnapping firsthand. It had been my job to look after her, to take care of her. And I'd really messed it up.

"They took Mags," I said, my voice trembling in the same way hers had upon the discovery of the bodies in the ice sculpture garden. "They took her, and they're gone." Fresh tears welled, and I choked back a sob as Nan wrapped her arms around me and made a soft shushing sound.

"Oh, dear. Dear. Dear. Dear," she repeated like a chant.

Her gentleman friend moved closer and placed a hand on Nan's shoulder. I hadn't even noticed his arrival earlier, but now here he was, pushing his way into this family moment.

"Who took her?" he asked in a deep rumble.

"I don't know." I kept my eyes on Nan

instead of looking toward Mr. Milton. "I couldn't see the face, but they put her into the back of a white van and drove away. I didn't even get the license plate number."

"Well, that's a rotten thing to do and not with keeping the spirit of the season either," Nan mumbled into my hair. "But we'll get her back, I promise."

I fell apart in my grandmother's arms, asking her the many frantic questions that swirled through my mind. "What if it was the same people who killed the judges? What if they're going to kill her, too? It's all my fault. She doesn't even know anyone here. I don't understand. Why would they take her? I mean, why would anyone want to take Mags, especially someone who doesn't even know her?"

A small paw patted the back of my calf. I turned around and bent down, expecting to find Paisley, but instead, it was Octo-Cat who sat there looking rather pleased with himself.

"Now that I've finally filled my stomach, I can think a little clearer," he explained, then stopped to lick his paw and drag it across his forehead. I waited impatiently as he licked and dragged—licked and dragged half a dozen times—without providing further commentary.

Finally I blurted out, "Do you know something? Do you know who took Mags?"

He dropped his paw back to the ground and stared up at me with large amber eyes.

"I don't know anything," Mr. Milton answered, assuming I'd been talking to him. How could I have forgotten he was here? I needed to be more careful with my secret, no matter how much I was worried about my cousin in that moment.

"Of course I don't know *that,*" Octo-Cat answered with an exasperated groan. "But I think I know something else that might help." He paused again for emphasis, the way he so often liked to do when he was building the drama of the scene.

My cat's love of theatrics would be the end of me one day. Quite literally. I'd probably have a heart attack while waiting out one of his dramatic pauses.

"Well?" I demanded, unable to take it anymore as I moved my hands to my hips. I shifted my eyes from the cat to Nan, pretending she was the target of my ire so that I'd at least have a cover in front of Mr. Milton.

Ugh. Why had she brought him along?

"*Yeesh.* So impatient." My cat stopped again and stared at me, challenging me to push him again.

I bit my tongue and waited him out while Nan filled the silence to keep up our charade.

After several moments, Octo-Cat seemed appeased and blinked his eyes slowly before continuing. "Even though you're being a bit rude, I'll tell you what I know. You know how all humans look the same? You and Mags look even more the same than most."

Even though I was pretty sure I knew what he was getting at, I asked for clarification, anyway. "What do you mean?"

Nan gave an answer, but my ears were focused firmly on Octo-Cat.

He shook his head, flicked his tail, and sighed yet again. "*I mean* whoever took Mags probably meant to take you instead. Think about it, and you'll see that I'm right. As usual."

CHAPTER EIGHT

The moment Octo-Cat spoke those words, I knew they were true. Mags didn't know anyone in Blueberry Bay besides my family and me.

No one had any reason to take her.

True, she had no friends here, but also no enemies.

Me, on the other hand… Well, let's just say I'd ruffled more than a few feathers during the course of my investigations. But was that enough for someone to want to kidnap me?

Rather than continue to puzzle over this myself, I decided to ask Nan. Even though I already knew I believed in Octo-Cat's theory, I still had a hard time wrapping my head around the fact that someone had meant me harm.

"Do you think the people who took Mags meant to take me instead? Everyone is always saying how similar we look, and well, maybe…" I let my voice trail off.

She bit her lip and nodded. "It would seem that way, wouldn't it?" she asked, shaking her head now.

Mr. Milton wrapped an arm around Nan's shoulders and pulled her tight into his side. The familiarity of this gesture made my stomach turn over.

"Who would want to take her—or you—so badly that they'd risk doing it in the middle of a crowded festival?" he asked, his eyes boring into mine.

Although that was an appropriate question, it still rankled me. I wished Nan would ask Mr. Milton to go away and leave the investigation to us.

He was also wrong. The streets had begun to fill out a bit more as the morning wore on, but we still didn't have anything near a crowd, especially in the mostly empty area that housed the ice sculpture garden outside of the main action.

Scanning the streets, I did a quick count and noticed four people in the nearby vicinity. If they'd seen what happened with the van, they certainly weren't letting on. Those who had witnessed my frantic run had already departed, more than likely not realizing how serious matters had become.

Nan remained cuddled up against Mr. Milton, although the lovey-dovey look she'd had in her eyes earlier had long since flown the coop.

"It wouldn't be that hard to sneak in and out with a plan," she pointed out. "People will be coming and going all day, there's parking in at least half a dozen different places, and many vendors are bringing their vans and SUVs in to load and unload. So, you see, it would be relatively easy to take her. Easier than it normally would be, at least."

"We're going with my theory, then. Right?" Octo-Cat asked impatiently. "Because I'm right about this, just like I'm right about most things. Really, you need to start listening a bit quicker."

I nodded in response. While I also hated to waste time discussing already established points, I also couldn't trust everything he said at face value. Not only was he often crabby and sarcastic, but some of his ideas were a bit too influenced by the melodramatic TV shows he liked watching before and after his morning and afternoon naps.

Octo-Cat sniffed the cold air above his head. "Are you answering me or simply humoring me? It's so much harder when you're not talking to me. Are we proceeding with the assumption that you were the target instead of Mags?"

"Yes," I hissed partially under my breath. It's like he didn't care about keeping my secret at all.

"What was that?" Mr. Milton asked with a furrowed brow and a quizzical expression.

"Oh, *uh,* just talking to myself," I stuttered as heat flushed my cheeks. "What I meant was *yes, Nan's absolutely right.* Anyone could have taken her, and the longer we wait to go after her, the harder it will be to find her. We need to do something, and we need to do it now."

Nan wriggled free of his arm. "Yes, yes, we need to go after her."

"But she could be anywhere," Mr. Milton said with a sigh. "Someone dangerous could have her. We could be walking into a situation that we might not walk out of."

I glowered at him, hating that he had any say in this at all.

"It's what family does," I said. "It's what good people do. They show up. They help each other."

"Especially at Christmastime," Nan added, making a tsking noise as she shook her head dolefully. "It's what we're going to do."

"Yeah, and if you're not up for it, we can handle this ourselves," I added, hoping that he would take the bait and make a run for it.

He cleared his throat and fixed his eyes on me with a bit of a grimace. "Well, I can't leave you two lovely ladies on your own, especially when the situation could be dangerous."

I shrugged. "Suit yourself."

Then I turned toward Nan, intentionally

facing away from Mr. Milton. "The first thing we need to do is call Mom and Dad and make sure they know what's going on. We'll need everybody working hard to find Mags— and let's not forget, the ice sculpture murderer."

"What a Holiday Spectacular this is turning out to be," Nan pointed out grimly.

She turned to the side and faced Mr. Milton. "Would you please give us a moment, dear?" she asked with a slight smile.

"Oh yes. Oh yes, of course. I'll just go get us some latkes. They looked good, and perhaps a hot snack is just what we all need now." He stumbled away, clearly sore about Nan's dismissal, but I was happy she'd done it and hoped she planned to avoid him during the rest of our search as well.

Her eyes flashed as she turned them on me, speaking quietly and quickly. "I'll take care of the call to your folks," she said. "You see what the animals know."

"Already on it," I said, nodding just once before scooping both animals up in my arms to Paisley's delight and Octo-Cat's disdain.

"Listen up, guys," I said. "There are

people down the block, so I can't be too loud, and if anyone comes close, I might have to quiet up mid-sentence. Okay? Let's chat. Did you hear anything? Or see anything? Or smell anything that can help us find out what happened to Mags?"

Octo-Cat shifted into a more comfortable position but still seemed put off by being clutched to my chest beside the wagging ball of Paisley. "They do this to cats all the time, you know. Come in vans, take us away, put us in the pound. I've never had to deal with such indignities, obviously, but nobody calls for reinforcements when it happens to us."

Paisley whined and dipped her head. "It happened to me. That's how I got to the shelter in the first place. After my first mom died, me and my brothers and sister were living in the street and so hungry we didn't know what we were going to do. But then a big van came and took us to the shelter. It wasn't quite as bad there, but then Nan came and found me, and everything was perfect, and it's been perfect ever since."

Octo-Cat rolled his eyes at her. "If you're suggesting that Mags is better off because some random hooded guy in a van took her, then you would be very, very wrong. It doesn't work the same way for humans as it does for us."

Paisley whimpered again. "But you said if it were a cat…"

"I know what I said. Sometimes I just need to give Angela a hard time, so she knows I'm paying attention."

Now I rolled my eyes.

"Paisley, sweetie," I said softly, "thank you for telling me your story, but in this case, Octo-Cat is right. Whoever took Mags doesn't want to help her."

"Are they going to hurt her?" the little dog asked, shaking violently at the prospect

"I hope not," I said in a strained whisper.

At the same time, Octo-Cat answered, "Yeah, probably."

I choked back a sob.

If something happened to Mags, I'd never forgive myself. Not just because she'd come to Glendale on my account, but because the kidnapper had most likely meant to take me instead.

Would he be angry when he realized Mags was the wrong person?

Would he come for me, too?

Would he dispose of her?

Let her go?

Oh, how I wished I knew.

CHAPTER NINE

Mr. Milton returned with two orders of latkes about fifteen minutes after he first departed.

Nan accepted hers by giving him a quick peck on the cheek.

I shook my head and said, "No thanks," still clutching Octo-Cat tight.

Paisley had already jumped down to dance at Nan's feet.

Honestly, there was so much fear in my stomach already that I didn't have much room for anything else.

They made quick work of their snack while I racked my brain trying to figure out how best to proceed. "I'm going to go find

Mr. Gable," I announced before heading decisively to the right, leaving them both behind.

"Mommy! Mommy! I'm coming, too!" Paisley cried, frolicking after Octo-Cat and me in her silly reindeer costume.

We found Mr. Gable in the same place I left him earlier that morning—at the main entry to the festival dressed up as a jacketless Santa while guiding visitors into his sleigh for the perfect photo op.

His bunny sidekick E.B. sat nearby in the nativity scene half covered in hay and looking hilariously out of place as a life-size bunny nestled among miniature plastic shepherds, wisemen, cows, camels, and angels.

Mr. Gable finished with the family of four he was photographing, wished them a Merry Christmas, and then turned toward me, concern furrowing his brow.

"Why, Angie... Why do you look so out of breath? Are you coming from the latest reindeer game?" He chuckled in that soft, happy way that old men had, but not quite vibrant or boisterous enough to match his role as Santa.

Once again I was reminded that I needed to make some effort to get into better shape, especially since my seventy-year-old Nan could run circles around me—and often did.

"Mr. Gable, have the police been in touch with you?" I drew out my phone and looked at the time displayed on its screen. Surprisingly, little more than half an hour had passed since I'd told officer Bouchard about my discovery of the two corpses in the ice sculpture garden and even less time than that since Mags was taken.

Mr. Gable's cheeks turned red to match mine. Now he looked more like Santa, which made me happy somehow. "Why would the police have been in touch? What happened?"

As much as I didn't want to be the one to tell him, it looked like I had no choice. I caught him up on the discovery of the bodies and that we already knew at least one was a judge his committee had hired. I also told him how Mags had been kidnapped shortly after and hauled away in a speeding cargo van.

He stared at me for a moment, eyes wide and unblinking. "All that happened this

morning? Right here at our Holiday Spectacular?" His voice cracked on that last syllable.

"Afraid so," I answered with a frown.
"Officer Bouchard is taking care of things at
the crime scene. He's already called for
backup and I'm trying to figure out who took
Mags and how I can get her back."

That was one problem with living in a
small town. We didn't really have enough
cops to handle the double homicide, let alone
a kidnapping on top of that. That's why my
work as a private investigator was so important. Officer Bouchard had let me partner
with him on investigations more than once for
this very reason.

"What should we do?" Mr. Gable asked,
his face turning from red to white to red
again, a flashing display of his anxiety.

"We've been planning the Spectacular all
year. Vendors have come from all over Blueberry Bay. Folks travel from out of town to be
here. Hundreds more are on their way right
now. Do we close everything down and call it
a loss, or do we try to keep going despite the
crimes that were committed here this
morning?"

I shook my head, wishing I had an answer. "Seems like a lose-lose, no matter what you do. I wouldn't want to be in your position."

He sighed heavily and ran both hands through his thick white hair. "Ugh. This was not a responsibility I thought I'd ever have as chairman of the committee. But even if I'm the head, we are a team. I think I need to let the others weigh in before I make a definitive decision. Wouldn't you say?"

I set Octo-Cat down on the front seat of the sleigh and then joined him on the bench.

Paisley pranced below, too short to hop up for herself. So I bent over and gave her a lift. She immediately licked my face, happy to be reunited after our fifteen-second separation.

"That sounds like a good plan to me," I said, largely because I had no other ideas to offer. "I'll stay here to greet people and take their pictures while you go talk with the others."

"Oh, wonderful, wonderful," he said, pushing the sleek digital camera into my hands. "Would you mind watching E.B. too? She'll probably just sleep through everything.

I have her leash tied to that back camel's leg there, so she shouldn't give you any trouble."

"Of course we'll keep an eye on her. No problem at all," I assured him.

"Bunny-sitting duty? Gag me," Octo-Cat moaned beside me.

Mr. Gable smiled quickly, but the slight look of happiness disappeared from his face in an instant, and he rushed off muttering something to himself.

I glanced toward the nearest parking lot but couldn't see any new festivalgoers arriving. That meant I had a small bit of privacy and could talk to the animals again.

"I thought we were going to find Mags," Paisley whined.

"That is what she said we were going to do," Octo-Cat added. "But you know how fickle humans can be. Angela, how long are we going to be stationed here, away from the action?"

I wished I knew. There were a lot of things I wished I knew right about then, and only one new creature I could ask for information.

I slipped down from the sleigh's bench

seat and tiptoed toward the nativity display, careful not to disturb the rabbit. From last I remembered meeting her, she was a very nervous sort and I needed to see if she knew anything that could help me. If I frightened her, though, chances were she wouldn't talk to me at all.

I needed to play this exactly right.

For Mags.

CHAPTER TEN

O nce I reached the nativity display, I
sat down gently beside the manger.
An icy dampness immediately saturated my
bottom, but I didn't care.

"E.B.," I said softly. "E.B., it's me, Angie.
We met at the pet shop when we were there
for pictures with Santa. I don't know if you
remember me, but—"

The hay beside me twitched, and a little
gray nose poked its way out, followed by two
dark eyes. "Oh my gosh, oh my gosh. Who
are you? What are you doing here? Where's
Mr. Gable? Are you going to eat me? Am I
going to die? Is everything okay? Oh Merry
Christmas, what a Christmas…"

Octo-Cat appeared at my side with a snarky grin stretched between his whiskers. I couldn't tell whether he was here to help me or to have some fun at E.B.'s expense.

"Relax, rabbit," he snarled. "She's not going to eat you. But if you don't cooperate, maybe I will."

He laughed devilishly in the same way he did when he threw up outside my bedroom door, enjoying the means much more than the end. So he'd be helping me and making things more difficult at the exact same time. *Great.*

"Oh, Merry Christmas, Merry Christmas!" E.B. sputtered, using the holiday greeting as a curse word. "I do not want to be eaten. I do *not*. I knew I shouldn't have left home today. Mr. Gable made me, but I didn't want to go. I just wanted to sleep at home and eat carrots, and oh!"

With a wildly flicking tail, my cat shouted, "If you know what's good for you, you'll listen to what the lady has to say. No more of this 'Merry Christmas' business. You got me?"

The bunny nodded slowly, her long ears flopping in the hay. "I'm sorry," she sputtered in fear. "I didn't mean to make you angry, Mr. Cat. It's just… I always have to be on alert or bad things can happen. Life isn't so easy when you're prey, you know? Anybody here could hurt me. Lots of bunnies don't get the chance to live as long as I've lived already, and I want to keep on living. I love my human."

Paisley joined us now. I had no idea where she'd been the last couple minutes, but we still seemed to be free of any newly arriving visitors, so I pressed on.

"Do you—" I began, but Paisley interrupted me, which was very uncharacteristic of her.

She let out a sad howl. Now her normally erect ears fell forward as she tilted her head and studied the bunny with an expression of sorrow. "Oh, you poor bunny. I can't imagine what life is like for you. Do you want to talk about it? I'm a very good listener."

I was just about to say something to get us back on topic when an increasingly perturbed Octo-Cat came to my rescue.

"Once again, this isn't the Dr. Phil show, and we're not here to talk about the bunny's feelings. We need information. We need to find Mags. Keep your eye on the prize. Keep your head in the game. Yada yada. And all those other favorite human clichés, too. Now," he said, turning back to E.B. with flashing yellow eyes. "One of our humans has been kidnapped by dangerous men."

The bunny gasped.

"*Yes*," said Octo-Cat dramatically, nodding as he did. "*Dangerous*. And we need to get her back before it's too late."

He took two quick steps forward and unsheathed the claws on one paw demonstratively. "Now tell us what you know, rabbit."

The bunny's nose never stopped wiggling even as the rest of her body grew still with fright. "I don't know what you expected of me," she said weakly. "I'm sorry something happened to your human, but I don't know anything about it. Now, please, can I get back to my nap?"

Octo-Cat licked his exposed claws while narrowing his eyes on the rabbit. I hadn't realized my cat was such a mafioso when it came to the pets of Glendale. I'd have to monitor his television-viewing habits a bit more carefully, it seemed.

He began to speak, but I cut him off by placing a hand on his back. "More flies with honey than vinegar," I mumbled.

"Who would want flies?" the tabby asked. "Disgusting and completely off topic."

I rolled my eyes and focused them on E.B. "You've been here all morning watching as everyone comes and goes. Did you see anyone acting suspicious?"

"I see everything," E.B. said with a nod before freezing up again. "That's the difference between staying alive and becoming a snack."

"Okay..." I said slowly, given that she hadn't actually deigned to answer my question. "Did you see anyone suspicious?"

One of her ears twitched, then the other. "I find every predator suspicious," she said. "Including you. And especially that cat."

Octo-Cat laughed gaily as if this was the best thing he'd ever heard as well as all he'd ever wanted for Christmas.

"I understand," I said slowly, once again hoping Mr. Gable wouldn't get back soon so we could pursue more productive means of inquiry. "Was anyone more suspicious than the others? Or suspicious in a different way?"

E.B. thought about this. "Well," she said at last. "Now that you mention it, yes. I did see some suspicious humans come through."

Now we were getting somewhere.

CHAPTER ELEVEN

"Do you know who took Mags?" Paisley asked, wagging her tail hopefully as we all stared at E.B. waiting to find out what she knew.

"Who's Mags?" the bunny asked distract-edly. "Your human just asked me if I saw anyone suspicious."

"Yes, that's right," I jumped in to steer the conversation back to the right path. "Tell me about those suspicious people."

E.B. tentatively lifted one ear, then set it back down. "Lots of people have come through, and almost everyone stopped to say hello to Mr. Gable and get their picture taken, but a couple people seemed in too much of a hurry."

"So you're saying they refused to have their picture taken?" I asked to make sure I understood.

"They didn't even let him ask. It was very strange to see a predator behave in that way. One of them was looking all around, back and forth, like I do when I'm trying to figure out if danger is nearby. The other moved very quickly and raced right past us without so much as a hello."

"That is strange," I agreed thoughtfully. "Can you tell me anything more about those two people? Did they come together? What did they look like? Did you recognize them?"

E.B. blinked slowly and wiggled her nose. "Everyone else got their picture taken, but not those two. They didn't come at the same time, either. First one came, then some time passed, and then the other. I don't know who they were."

"Do you know, if they were male or female? Old or young? Can you describe how they looked?"

E.B. turned her head slightly, eyeing Octo-Cat for a moment before returning her attention to me. "I don't know. All humans look the same, really. You don't even have any special markings on your coats to help show the difference. It makes it hard to tell you apart."

"Exactly," Octo-Cat said, nodding. "Isn't that what I've always said?"

E.B. flinched. "That's all I know. I don't know anything else. Please will you go away now?"

"Thank you for your help," I told her, rising to my feet and dusting a light smattering of hay from my bottom, which by now was soaked completely through from the melting snow on the ground. So much for the hay creating a drying buffer. "We told Mr. Gable we'd watch you, but we can do that from a little bit farther away."

"Thank you," she murmured, watching us warily as we left the nativity scene.

"Well that was pointless," Octo-Cat hissed. If I'd taken the moment to look over to him, I'm sure I'd have seen him rolling his eyes. "I'm so glad we took time to ask the bunny."

"There's a lot of things she did help us with," I pointed out, raising the camera in one hand. "E.B. mentioned that there were two suspicious people and that neither had their photo taken."

"So what do you suggest we do?" Octo-Cat asked with a flick of his tail. "Look through all the photos on that thing and cross reference it with everyone who's attended the festival so far?"

"For a start," I said, impressed he had understood with no explanation on my part. Then again, he was becoming quite savvy with photography given his long-distance Instagram relationship with Grizabella.

"There's more than one entrance into this place," I continued on. "People can start from anywhere. There are, no doubt, many people who didn't stop for a photo who perhaps never even made their way over here."

"*And,*" Octo-Cat added, his amber gaze fixed on me knowingly,

"what's suspicious to the rabbit might not be suspicious at all. So there were two people she thought were acting funny, but it's possible that neither of them had anything to do with the murders or the kidnapping."

"I know," I said with a sigh, "but at least it's a place to start."

I powered the camera back on and flipped through the last few photos on display. Before I could make it very far, however, several people converged on us at once.

Nan and her gentleman friend, Mr. Milton, came from one direction while Mr. Gable returned from another. Lastly, my boyfriend, Charles, approached as well, immediately slinging an arm over my shoulder and giving me a kiss on my forehead.

"I finished up my work early at the firm and thought I'd surprise you," he said with a giant grin. "So tell me, what did I miss?"

Mr. Gable groaned, Nan winced, and Mr. Milton looked pointedly at the ground.

Octo-Cat had an answer for him, but it was one he couldn't decipher without my help. Also it wasn't very nice.

Paisley barked and stood on her hindlegs, doing her sit pretty dance to get Charles's attention.

"Hey," he said, lifting her into his arms and giving her a kiss on the forehead, too.

"Why is everyone so quiet?" he asked, his eyes darting around our impromptu circle. "I really did miss something, didn't I?"

I put a hand on his shoulder and gently informed him both of the murders and the kidnapping as well as the fact that we were pretty convinced the kidnappers meant to nap me instead of Mags.

"All that in one morning?" he asked with an empty expression.

I nodded sadly. "I don't know what to do," I moaned. "Do you have any ideas?"

Mr. Gable cleared his throat. "I've spoken with the other committee members, and we all think it would be best to shut down the festival. We're circulating word to the vendors now and giving them the option of setting up at the local park. We'll man the exits and send anyone who comes by over there instead while the police are doing their thing."

Mr. Milton nodded and raised a thumb and finger to his chin. "Lots to lose, canceling the biggest event of the year. Vendors aren't going to be too happy about that."

"They'll lose money," Nan agreed, "but at least they won't lose their lives."

"That's the goal," Mr. Gable agreed.

"Come on," Charles said. "Let's go find Mags."

And even though I didn't need my boyfriend to save the day, I was very glad he was now here at my side.

We would find Mags. We would.

I wouldn't accept any other outcome.

CHAPTER TWELVE

"Do you think the crimes are linked?" Charles asked me matter-of-factly as I led him toward the spot where Mags had been abducted. He carried Paisley while I carried Octo-Cat, who had the good grace not to complain this time.

"I just don't know," I answered, keeping my eyes on the ground as if it held some answer we had yet to discover. "I don't think they are, but I also don't want to overlook anything. Just in case."

"Good thinking," Charles said, squeezing my elbow since I required both of my hands to carry Octo-Cat comfortably, lest I wanted his complaining to pick up again. "I'm sorry I wasn't here earlier," Charles said.

"That's okay. You didn't know. How could *anyone* know these terrible things would happen? And on Christmas Eve, too…"

Charles remained quiet for the next half block, becoming lost in thought as he so often did. "Do you think it's possible they happened not despite it being Christmas Eve but *because* it's Christmas Eve?"

"What you mean?" I asked, risking a glance at him even though I needed to keep both eyes on the street in order to avoid bumping into one of the many departing vendors.

"Well, maybe the Holiday Spectacular gave our murderer and/or kidnapper an opportunity he wouldn't have otherwise had. Or maybe the murderer is somehow related to the festival itself. You said the victims were meant to judge the ice sculpture contest. Right?"

"Well, at least one of them," I answered. Thinking back, Officer Bouchard didn't recognize the woman, and I hadn't been back to chat with him because of what had happened to Mags.

"I know every second counts right now," Charles told me as we neared the ice sculpture garden, "but let's take a quick moment to check in with the police. They may have information that could help point us in the right direction for Mags, too."

Less than two minutes later, we found Officer Bouchard standing with a couple other police personnel near the giant Christmas tree sculpture. "Angie," he said. "I'm surprised you weren't back before now."

"Didn't you hear? I asked, my voice dry and itchy. "Somebody took Mags. Kidnapped her right off the street."

"Mags? Your nice cousin? But why?" His eyebrows pressed together. "And why wasn't I informed before now?"

That was right. We hadn't even stopped to inform the authorities of Mags's abduction. Nan had probably assumed I would do it while I assumed she would. At least I could tell my favorite police officer now.

"It's all been a blur," I admitted "I can't

believe I forgot to come to you, but I know you've been busy over here."

He sighed and rolled a kink from his neck. "Busy is an understatement."

"Learn anything new?" Charles asked, shaking the officer's hand hello. "Anything that might help us find Mags while you hunt the killer?"

"*Hunt*'s not exactly an appropriate word. Sounds like somebody's been reading too many Stephen King novels," the officer quipped. "But yes, we were able to confirm that the female victim was our second judge. A Miss Zelda Benedict. She taught art at the university in Portland and drove up special to serve as our judge."

I sucked air in through my teeth. This just kept getting worse and worse. "What a way for us to make a good impression on outsiders. *Come to Glendale's Holiday Spectacular where you just might get murdered.*"

"It is unfortunate," Officer Bouchard agreed. "She was very well respected in her field. Her colleagues will no doubt ride us hard until we find out who the culprit is."

"Did she have any connection to Fred Hapley?"

"As far as I know, the two of them never met a day in their life. At least not until they wound up dead side-by-side in the snow here. By the way, the murder weapon for old Fred was a gun. It must've had a silencer since no one reported hearing anything. But Zelda? She was stabbed straight through with an icicle."

"Why not kill them both the same way?" Charles asked, wrapping an arm protectively around my waist and eyeing the nearby ice sculptures warily.

"That's what we wondered, too," Officer Bouchard said with a nod. "Seems to me that somebody had come prepared to commit one murder but then had to commit a second when Fred here walked in on the scene."

"So we're looking for someone who knew the festival well enough to plan a private moment with Zelda Benedict in the ice sculpture garden before most of the tourists arrived and the scene got busy. But also someone who didn't know the agenda well enough to anticipate Fred Hapley's arrival," Charles summarized.

"That's what we're thinking." Officer Bouchard bobbed his head and reached over to give Paisley a quick pat. "But now you tell me someone took your cousin, too. She didn't arrive on the scene until after both judges were slain and the murderer had disappeared. So why would someone take her?"

"The murderer disappeared from view, but maybe he stayed close to keep an eye on things," I ventured, hugging Octo-Cat tight to my chest for strength. "Maybe he watched us the entire time as we discovered the bodies, talked with you, and then got ready to guard. But then why wouldn't he take me too?"

"Unfortunately, we've got a lot of questions and very few answers so far." Officer Bouchard hung his head and sighed. "I'll call Mags's kidnapping in to the station. Even though our men are occupied with the homicide scene here, the neighboring police forces are all on standby given the size of our event, and the folks in Dewdrop Springs have dealt with their fair share of kidnappings over the years. They really are the experts on that kind of thing while murders are becoming far too common in our little town."

"Thank you for your help," I mumbled, hating everything about how this day was turning out.

"I wish there was more I could do. But if I know you, you're already halfway to finding her yourself."

We said goodbye, then Charles, the animals, and I headed toward the spot where I'd last seen Mags before she was hauled away and this whole nightmare had gone from bad to worse.

Hopefully we would find a definitive clue soon. I still didn't know where to go in the search for my lost cousin, and as time ticked steadily on, my heart sunk lower and lower.

"Please, God," I mumbled in a nearly silent prayer, looking toward the sky as fat snowflakes fell to the earth. "Please let her be okay."

CHAPTER THIRTEEN

E ven though the snowfall had remained light that morning, it had also been consistent. That meant the footprints I'd left when I chased after the van that took Mags had already mostly filled in with fresh fall. Nearly a dozen other pairs of prints wove through the street and around the block, too, adding a new layer of difficulty to retracing my steps.

More and more people had begun to arrive for the festival, only to be turned right back around and sent on their way. Could this be the end of their town's most favorite tradition?

No, that doesn't matter now.

"This is where they took her," I told Charles, motioning toward an alley that cut between the shops. "He pulled through there, and then I lost track of him."

"I chased them, too!" Paisley interjected proudly. "But my little legs were no match for that big, bad van."

Sometimes I wondered whether my Chihuahua thought other humans could understand her, too. Either that or she just felt it was polite to talk to everyone, whether or not they had any idea what she was saying.

"The snow has filled in most of the tire tracks, but I still see some slight grooves." Charles stooped down and touched the ground. "Let's follow them as far as we can and see where that gets us."

"The kidnappers weren't the only ones to have a car," Octo-Cat grumbled within my arms. "We're in the middle of downtown. Practically everyone has a car. That's how we got here. UpChuck, too."

"Thanks for that observation," I told my cat, thankful for the relative privacy of the alley.

"What's he saying?" Charles asked, both eyebrows raised.

He definitely knew that Octo-Cat talked bad about him. After all, I was the one who had revealed my cat's nickname for the guy was *UpChuck*. Still, I hated translating all the sarcastic barbs that came from my naughty kitty's mouth.

"Uh... nothing," I said slowly, glancing down the alley and hoping to spot something that would help change the subject—preferably something that would also help lead us to Mags.

"I can tell when he's being mean, you know," Charles said with a self-effacing chuckle.

"What?" I stopped to study him for any signs that he was joking at my expense, but his expression remained serious as he met my gaze. "How could you possibly know something like that?"

Charles shrugged and put an arm around my waist.

Paisley now skittered before us, leaving his arms free while Octo-Cat preferred to stay in mine and avoid the damp snow.

"I don't know. I can just tell. Maybe it's all the time I spend with Jacques and Jillianne, now that I've become a cat owner myself, or maybe I'm just getting to know him and his ways."

"You don't think you can..." My voice trailed off. This question was almost too crazy to ask, but if Charles really could understand Octo-Cat's tone when he was being facetious, maybe he could...

"Do you understand him?" I asked, placing eerie emphasis on each word in that sentence.

"No," he responded, chuckling again. "I wouldn't want to, either. It's one thing to know he says bad things about me and it's quite another to hear them for myself. Especially when we're all trying to work together to solve the case. And especially when it's Mags."

Charles had come to hang out with us a couple times since Mags's arrival and the two had hit it off splendidly—the way Charles did with everyone.

Beyond that, I knew he just wanted me to be happy and to make sure nothing bad happened to the people I loved. He was a good guy, Charles Longfellow, III. He never wanted anyone to get hurt. That's what made him such an expert lawyer. He went the extra mile for his clients every single day.

"Mommy! Mommy!" Paisley woofed, running back toward me so fast she looked like a tiny reindeer blur on the horizon.

I'd been so preoccupied with Charles's revelation I hadn't even realized she'd pulled ahead.

"Mommmmmmmyyyyyyyyyy!" she shouted again, drawing out the word for a couple extra beats. "I smell it! I smell her!"

"What do you smell, sweetie?" I asked, trying not to get my hopes up. Paisley always tried her best to help in whatever way she could, but her natural lack of suspiciousness made her a poor sleuth.

The dog had now reached us and was wagging her tail so hard I thought she might fall over. Even though I knew Nan preferred to keep her Chihuahua companion dressed while she was out on the town, I decided to free Paisley of her over-the-top costume.

She'd be much more of a help to all of us if she wasn't in constant danger of toppling over. Just like the Grinch's dog when he, too, had been dressed unceremoniously as a reindeer.

"Thank you, Mommy," she said with a happy sigh, shaking out her fur in the same way she did right after a bath. Hopefully, she wouldn't start zipping around like a maniac and rolling around in a frantic blur, which were the next two steps in her post-bath celebration.

"That feels much better," she said, then shook again but thankfully resisted taking her happy dance any farther. "Do you want to know what I smell?"

"I can tell you what she smells," Octo-Cat said from within my arms, a slight purr rising from his striped form. "It's those fried potato things."

"*Hey,*" the little dog whined. "I wanted to be the one to say. I wanted to help Mommy, so she would tell me I'm a good dog."

"You are the very best dog, Paisley, and don't worry, you can still tell me. Go ahead."

Octo-Cat had discovered this clue and chosen to keep it to himself. As far as I was concerned, Paisley was the one who deserved all the praise here.

She rolled on the ground once and then popped back up and sang, "It's the la-la-lokis. Or the latlatkes? I forget, but Mags ate a lot of them. She gave me a little piece, but I didn't like it. I think I would've rather had a lobster roll like Octo-Cat."

This piqued the cat's interest. "They do make a mighty fine lobster roll at the Little Dog Diner. Mighty fine. Shall we have another before heading home?"

"Not the time," I scolded him. "So you smell the food that Mags was eating just before she was taken?"

Paisley nodded and then stumbled slightly to the side, apparently needing to get used to being out of the costume just as she'd needed to get used to being in it. "Yeah, I smell it and it's going this way." She spun in a full circle and then ran down the alley and turned.

"Let's go," I said, shoving Octo-Cat into Charles's arms because I knew he could run faster and easier with the extra burden than I could. I also didn't want to take the chance my cat would disappear if left unsupervised.

Nothing mattered other than getting to my cousin.

Well, at least not to three of the four members of our little search committee.

We all jogged.

The Chihuahua kept moving fast but occasionally lapped us while yelling high-pitched words of encouragement. "Mommy, you can do it! You're a good runner! Yes, you are! You're a good girl! Come on, Mommy!"

While I found her cheerleading cute, it wasn't entirely helpful. At last, when my legs had begun to feel a bit prickly from all the unplanned movement in my tight jeans, Paisley stopped, let out a low growl, and stood with her head angled slightly toward the ground.

Charles and I slowed.

"Well, that was terrible," Octo-Cat complained. "Let's not do that again. Shall we?"

I ignored him and followed Paisley's line of sight with both my eyes and my feet.

"Do you see, Mommy?" the Chihuahua asked, impossibly keeping perfectly still despite the obvious desire to wag her tail hard. "This spot smells a lot like cousin Mags."

Charles and I both bent down to examine the fallen items that were partially covered in snow.

"That's because these are Mags's things," I revealed with a little gasp. I lifted her fuzzy white beret, discarded cell phone, and the shiny silver menorah she'd only just purchased that morning with shaky hands.

"Why did she leave them here?" Paisley asked with a little whine.

"I don't think she wanted to." I stowed all three items in my shoulder bag. "No. I don't think she wanted to," I repeated.

"So what do we do now?" Octo-Cat asked.

At the same time, Charles said, "Well, this is concrete evidence, and that's always a great thing to have."

"But what do we do now?" I parroted Octo-Cat's question.

"Why, we call in the cavalry, of course," came his response.

I loved Charles's ability to stay calm and level-headed, no matter how hard the going got. Even my cat had become fully invested in pursuing our case, his complaints coming out fewer and farther between. We were now working as one, and that made us unstoppable.

Mags, hang on. We're coming!

CHAPTER FOURTEEN

Charles called Nan while I called my mom.

She picked up on the first ring. "Hey, honey. Did you find Mags?"

"Not yet," I answered sadly. "But we have a small lead. Can you and Dad meet us at the alley off Third Street? You know the one right next to the pancake place?"

"Yes, we're coming!" she promised before hanging up.

Charles wrapped both arms around me and mumbled into my hair. "It's going to be okay. We'll find her. Your Nan is on the way right now, and she said something about bringing along a friend to help with the search."

"That will be Mr. Milton," I said, my voice coming out cold.

"Who's that? I don't think I've met him before."

"Neither had I. Not until today. It just seems weird, him hanging around with all that's going on."

"Well, maybe he really likes your Nan and wants to help in order to make her happy," Charles offered with shrug as he let me go.

I shook my head, unwilling to buy that, especially given his reaction earlier. "Yeah, or maybe he's the murderer we're all looking for."

Charles tutted. "You don't really believe that, do you?"

"Yes. No... I don't know. It just seems weird to me."

"Well, if you're not sure about him, then I'm not either. Maybe we can try asking him some questions when he arrives."

"Maybe."

"Are you talking about Nan's new friend?"

Octavius asked, curling his upper lip in disgust. At least we agreed on this one. "That guy doesn't have the missing parts to kill somebody."

"The missing parts?" I asked in confusion.

"Yeah, you know. The ones that boy kittens have before they go to the doctor and—"

"I got it!" I rushed to cut him off before he could add to that description.

"Still, he's rather suspicious to me," my tabby added. "Did you see a picture of him on Mr. Gable's camera when you looked?"

"The camera! That's right," I said, slapping my forehead. We'd totally forgotten to look through the images. "I'll just call Mr. Gable and see if he's willing to let us borrow that real quick."

Although the committee head was too busy to talk for long, he revealed that he'd handed the camera over to the police before begging off the call.

"See," Charles said, keeping his arms tight around me while Octo-Cat sat in the snow silently. "Someone's looking into it. We have lots of people helping find Mags."

"To be fair, I don't think Mr. Milton took Mags, but he could be the murderer. I don't know. It's just strange that a guy we've never met before has suddenly become so involved in our business."

Charles didn't say anything until Mom and Dad arrived a few minutes later.

They hugged Charles hello.

"That was quick," he said.

"We weren't too far away. Just over at the ice sculpture garden with the Officer Bouchard and the others. You'll be happy to know that they have the entire Dewdrop Springs and Misty Harbor police departments both out looking for Mags while the Glendale crew continues with the double homicide."

"Isn't that great?" Dad said with his signature oversized grin. "The more, the merrier. Also the more, the faster we'll find her. And we *will* find her, Angie."

I forced a smile. "Yeah, that's what everyone keeps saying. I sure hope you're all right."

"*Faith*. You gotta have it," Dad said, his smile stretching even wider.

"Listen," I said, dropping my voice low, making sure only the group of us could hear. "Before Nan comes by, I just wanted to say I don't trust that new friend she's taking everywhere with her."

"Are you saying you suspect *Mr. Milton?*" Mom asked, her voice hitching unnaturally high at the end of that question.

"I'm saying I don't know. But until we rule him out as a suspect, maybe. I mean, I don't know who he is. I don't know how well Nan knows him. Do you guys know anything about him?"

Mom ran her fingers through her hair as she thought. "I have met him once or twice while covering stories out on Caraway Island. He seems like a reasonably decent man."

Caraway Island. That was the one part of Blueberry Bay I seldom went. Not just because it required a ferry, but also because they didn't have much to offer other than beautiful scenery. And while ocean views and well-groomed beaches were perfectly nice, we all had those in our small corner of coastal Maine.

"Is there something wrong with Caraway

Island?" Charles asked, hooking an eyebrow in my direction. He'd become such a big part of my life since moving here about a year and a half ago that I sometimes forgot he originally hailed from California. He didn't know all the little quirks of living in Glendale yet.

"For one thing, the Caraway Island Cavaliers were our high school's biggest rival," I said, ticking off the first reason on my index finger, then raising a second finger as I continued with my list. "For another, folks from Glendale often visit Misty Harbor, Cooper's Cove, and Dewdrop Springs, and they all come over here, too. Those on the island mostly keep to themselves, like they're too good for the rest of us or something."

Geographically, Caraway Island was part of Blueberry Bay, but they didn't belong with us in any other way that counted. Perhaps that's why it felt so strange that Nan's new boyfriend—or whatever he was to her—hailed from the small, strange island.

"I wouldn't worry about it too much, Angie. I know we all have our little prejudices about those Cavaliers, but Nan likes Mr. Milton and she's a good judge of character,"

Mom offered, even though I wasn't sure she meant it.

"Maybe," I said looking away and still feeling so lost and defeated in all this.

"What else can you tell us? Has there been any progress?" Charles asked.

And if my parents hadn't been standing right there, I would've given him a big fat juicy kiss as a thank you for changing the subject.

"I've been staying right on the story of the *murders in the ice sculpture garden,*" Mom said, making her voice every bit as dramatic as Octo-Cat's was when he was telling the story or talking about himself. "The latest is that they found the statue the ice weapon was broken from. Even though it had mostly melted by the time the police arrived, they were still able to match it to a missing piece on the sculpture of a swan."

"I saw that one!" I said. "It's beautiful."

"It was beautiful, and it was made by Pearl from the animal shelter. You know Pearl, don't you? Well, let me just say she was devastated that her art had been used to kill that poor woman. Especially considering that she'd known Zelda Benedict and they were friendly."

"Do you think Pearl might have done it?" Charles ventured.

"Oh goodness, no!" Mom hissed, looking at Charles with shock and bewilderment. "Sweet Pearl is even older than Nan and not quite as spry. I have a hard time believing she can lift that five-pound Pomeranian of hers, let alone find the strength to first break off that giant icicle and then stab it through her friend's heart. Goodness me, not Pearl."

"What's everyone talking about over here?" Nan said, approaching with her usual swagger, arm linked in that of Mr. Milton.

"Thanks for coming so fast," Charles said, not wasting a second now that we were all together. "We found Mags's things spilled out on the ground here, so we know the kidnapper headed in this direction, and right now that's all we know. But it's a good place for us to start. Can you help us search?"

"I'll get the car," Dad said with a nod. "Meet you back here just as soon as I can."

"I'll get mine, too," Mr. Milton volunteered.

"And I'll go get mine," said Charles. "Angie, I'll be right back. Okay?"

"Okay," I nodded and accepted a quick kiss on the cheek.

As my boyfriend ran off with the other two men, Mom and Nan closed in for a group hug. We'd always been big huggers, but we took it to the extreme when facing situations like this. Danger and drama were becoming far too common for us these days, and I hated that Mags had been sucked into that.

"Do you guys have any theories?" I asked, knowing they probably wouldn't but still hoping they did.

Nan tilted her head. "I still can't get over the fact that one of them was killed with an icicle and the other a bullet. That doesn't seem very well planned to me."

"It really doesn't," Mom agreed. "And there's nothing to connect Fred and Zelda other than the fact they were both victimized today."

"There is a lot to think about with the murders, and of course I want to get justice for them. But right now Mags is what's important," I reminded them. "Do you have any theories about her?"

"Only that they meant to take you instead," Nan said with a frown. "And it's not a theory I like very much."

"But they took her instead of outright killing her. That's got to be a good thing. Right?" Mom asked, looking between me and Nan waiting for one of us to offer up a bit of encouragement.

"I hope so," I said for what felt like the millionth time that morning. Until we had Mags back safe and sound, it was the only thing I had.

Hope.

CHAPTER FIFTEEN

Dad returned with his car first, and Charles arrived shortly thereafter.

"Okay," I told everyone before departing, though Mr. Milton had still not returned. "We're looking for a white cargo van. The license plate may be too muddy to read or maybe they've given the car a wash since then. The truth is we don't have anything more than that. It's a definite long shot, but right now it's all we have to go on."

"Right-o," Dad said, touching his index finger and thumb together to make the *okay* signal. "Let's go get our girl."

I opened the passenger side door to Charles's sedan, and Paisley hopped right in.

He picked her up and placed her on the back-seat while I sat down carefully and arranged Octo-Cat on my lap.

Although my cat was much better about riding in the car now, sometimes his claws would still dig into my thighs if the driver took turns too hard or went too fast.

As soon as I had my seatbelt pulled securely over my lap, Charles gunned it. "Which way do you want to turn?" he asked me, moving us along quickly toward the main road.

All I had now was intuition and what I hoped might turn out as lucky guesses. For whatever reason, something tugged me toward the left.

We drove slowly through the well-traf-ficked areas while scanning every parking lot for a sign of our white van.

"This isn't going to work," I said after a ten-minute period that seemed to drag on for an eternity. "If they were smart enough to orchestrate a kidnapping, then they're smart enough to get the heck out of Dodge."

"Maybe," Charles agreed, continuing to

maneuver the streets of Glendale unperturbed, "but we still have to try."

"You're right, you're right," I said, continuing to search in silence.

Octo-Cat surprised me by pressing his two front paws to the base of the window and joining our search. His fuzzy little head whipped back and forth with determination. *Would he be the one to find her?*

If we were still searching after dark, he likely would. After all, he was the only one of us who could see well in the dark.

Oh, how I hoped it wouldn't come to that!

The longer it took, the higher the risk to Mags. We should have had her by now. She shouldn't have ever been taken.

"Mommy," Paisley yipped from the backseat. "I can't see. I can't see, and I want to help."

"Has she spotted something?" Charles asked, answering her bark.

"No," I translated without pulling my eyes away from the street. "She can't see anything back there and wants to help."

Charles patted his lap with one hand. "Oh, well then come here, girl. C'mon."

Paisley didn't need to be told twice. She vaulted from the backseat into Charles's lap where she now stood with her paws against the door in the same position as Octo-Cat.

"There are so many cars!" she remarked. "But only one of them took Mags."

"Obviously," my cat droned, but Paisley ignored him.

Charles kept driving straight. If we didn't turn off, we would eventually wind up in Cooper's Cove. Might the kidnappers have taken Mags there?

My eyes strained and the left one began to twitch as I felt my pulse boom beneath it. My brain stayed equally busy. So much was going on, it had become difficult to keep my head straight.

Two people had been killed, but the murderer may have only meant to take a single victim. Mags was kidnapped shortly thereafter, but the kidnappers may have meant to take me instead. We didn't know if the same person— or persons—had committed both crimes or whether it was just a big ol' coincidence they occurred so close together. I had no idea who would want to take me, who would want to hurt the judges, or where Mags could be.

It all felt like far too much.

And while investigating murders was often harrowing, we weren't usually racing against a clock. The dead would stay that way, no matter how long it took us to solve the murders, but Mags could still be saved.

"I don't like it when you do that," Octo-Cat said, turning to look back at me, a sneer on his little kitty face.

"Do what?" I said innocently.

"When you get all panicky. I can smell it, and it's not a good smell."

"You mean my stress hormones?"

"Whatever you want to call them. They're pretty disgusting, and anyway, you always do so much better when you're able to look at a situation logically. The moment you start freaking out is the moment you're working with a disadvantage."

Well...

I was dumbfounded by the insight of his

observation and needed a moment to decide how to respond.

Octo-Cat, however, kept going. "We've solved how many cases together now? This has got to be number ten or something near that, and each of those times no matter what happened, you figured it out. Well, usually it was me who played the most instrumental role, but you were there, and you helped, just like good assistants do. You'd be of a lot more assistance to me now if you just took a moment to get a grip already. You can treat it like an episode of *Law & Order*. First, we need to solve the crime, and then we can worry about getting justice for the victims."

He hummed a melodic beat that I believed was meant to be the *Law & Order* sound—*dun dun*—and although I didn't think everything in our lives could be likened to an episode of his favorite show, this time my cat was absolutely right.

I'd let myself become too fixated on what could happen next. I needed to shift my focus to what we already knew, what had already happened, and then go forward from there.

Taking his advice, I took several deep,

steadying breaths as I reviewed the facts of both cases in my mind.

"What are you thinking about?" Charles asked from beside me, chancing a quick glance in my direction while we continued on the road to Cooper's Cove.

"I'm going over everything we know and trying to look at things logically rather than letting my worry for Mags cloud everything."

"So you're relaxing a little?" he asked with a slight grin.

"I'm still crazy worried," I admitted with a sigh, "but I need to put that aside for everyone's benefit. Octo-Cat reminded me of that."

Charles reached over and patted Octo-Cat's head while moving his other hand to the top of the steering wheel. "He's a good cat when he wants to be."

"Yes he is," I agreed, smiling over at the tabby. "Yes he is…"

"So tell me what you're thinking," Charles continued. "Any fresh insights?"

I stayed silent for a minute as I gathered all my thoughts. "I just don't see a way that the murders and kidnapping can be linked other than the location, which I believe is a coincidence."

"Makes sense," he said. "Go on."

"I don't even think that both of *the murders* were planned, so it would be a stretch to add *the kidnapping* on top of that."

"And you've made a lot of enemies over the last year and a half," Octo-Cat reminded me with a quick flick of his tail.

I told Charles what the cat had said, and my boyfriend chuckled. "That's what happens when you're the good guy. You always ruffle some of the bad guy's feathers"

Octo-Cat perked up at this analogy, but I focused on asking the next logical question. "But whose feathers would be ruffled enough to try to abduct me?"

"Hmm. Let's review. First, there were the folks involved with Ethel Fulton's demise and inheritance dispute."

Octo-Cat winced. Even though I knew he was happy living with me now, he still missed his original owner every day.

Charles continued to discuss the murderers and other criminals we'd played a role in apprehending, coming up with a list of more than a dozen potential suspects.

"Looks like the cat's right," he quipped. "A lot of people have cause to be very angry with you. But who would it benefit to take you now? They've already been caught. No changing that now."

"Most recently, Octo-Cat and I solved the murder on the train and the one in the pet store."

"The folks from the train were apprehended, correct?" Charles asked, raising an eyebrow in my direction.

"Yes, they're in jail and some of the others we've caught are, too."

Charles nodded thoughtfully. *"In jail* doesn't mean *not capable.* They could have lackies working for them for all we know."

"So, what you're saying is *we can't rule anybody out?"*

He shook his head sadly. "Nope. Not a single person."

My phone buzzed from the place where I'd dropped it in Charles's cup holder after getting in the car.

"It's Nan," I cried, quickly answering the call and putting it on speaker.

"Angie, dear!" she shouted into the phone. "It's Mags! They've found her! She's safe!"

Tears welled in my eyes. "Oh thank goodness… Thank goodness." We hadn't been too late after all.

"We're on our way," I promised Nan.

"So are we. We're all going back to the Glendale police station. See you there."

CHAPTER SIXTEEN

We reached the Glendale police station in record time.

Charles swore he didn't go a mile over the speed limit—being the law-abiding lawyer he was—but I'm pretty sure that when I had the chance to sneak a peek at the speedometer, we were going at least ten over.

Then again, all the police were occupied elsewhere as we made our journey toward Mags.

When we got there, Nan and Mr. Milton had already arrived on the scene, and from what I could tell, Mags had just been delivered to the station as well.

"Oh, thank goodness, you're all right," I

cried, rushing to hug her as tight as I could. A giant wracking sob tore through me once I had her safe in my arms.

We'd been so close to losing each other after only just having been reunited... And I'd been dangerously close to losing her for good.

My cousin stared at me through glassy, unblinking eyes, her face devoid of any rosiness as she regarded me.

"Now, now. Just give her a moment," the delivering officer commanded. "She's had quite the shock, this one."

I gulped and took a step back, willing my cousin to speak to me—but she remained perfectly quiet as the rest of us settled in at the station.

Mom and Dad arrived about five minutes after the rest of us and hugged Mags just as tightly as I had.

"Whoa," the officer said with a kind chuckle. "I hadn't realized we'd be hosting a family reunion right here at the station."

Mom shot him a cold look, but nobody said anything more. Not until Mags delicately cleared her throat and searched the small room until she found me.

"Angie," she said, her voice emotionless, disconnected. *"Angie,"* she repeated with added emphasis. "They didn't want me. They wanted you."

"I know," I answered with a nod.

Charles pressed in close, holding Octo-Cat in his arms.

Paisley had already been returned to Nan with a flurry of licks and cuddles.

Mags reached forward now to stroke Octo-Cat's soft, striped fur. "They kept calling me Russo," she said, "and I don't think they figured out that I'm not you."

"Who is *they?* And why did they take you?" As horrible as I felt that this had happened at all, it was even worse to know for sure that it had been my fault.

"I don't know," Mags answered with a frown. "They blindfolded me in the van and tied my hands behind my back. I never got a good look at either of them."

"How many were there? Were they male? Female?" I asked, praying that this would soon make sense so that Mags's kidnappers would have to pay for what they'd done.

"I'll be the one to ask questions here," the cop growled in warning. He was one I hadn't met before, probably from one of the officers from out of town. "If you'll just give us a moment—"

Mags raised her hand and interrupted him. "No, they're my family. I want them here. Anything you want to ask me, they can hear, too."

"Okay," the officer said, nodding once although he obviously didn't agree. "Let's start with a description of your kidnappers. How many were there? Male? Female? Any defining characteristics to their voices, anything you remember hearing or smelling?"

Those were questions I was going to ask too. Some of them I already had. It seemed important to the officer that he remain in charge, so I remained quiet.

Mags shook her head slowly. "From what I could tell, there were two. A man and woman. Remember, I couldn't see anything. Only hear. And when the man pulled me into the car, I still had my things with me. That morning I bought a solid metal menorah from the nice ladies at the Hanukkah tent and I used it to thwack him over the head as hard as I could. It wasn't enough to knock him out, though. That's when he took everything away and threw it out the window."

I reached into my bag and pulled out the things we had found in the snow. "We've got everything right here for you," I said, returning them to her. "And good job getting that hit in."

A small smile flitted across Mags's face, but it was gone just as quickly as it had arrived.

"They kept calling me Russo, and I didn't correct them because I didn't want to put you in danger, and I didn't know what they would do if they found out they had the wrong person. I was so scared, Angie."

"I know," I said, my voice cracking.

"They were so angry. They kept telling me to keep my nose out of places where it didn't belong. They said bad things would happen to me, much worse than this if I crossed them again."

"But who?" I asked, unable to contain a groan.

Enormous tears spilled from Mags's eyes. "I don't know. I wish I did, so I could warn you. All I know is they were mad, and they said they'd definitely be back if you didn't fall in line. What did they mean, Angie? What have you gotten into? Is it drugs?"

"Never!" I assured her, placing a hand on her shoulder and giving it a squeeze. "This has to be related to my work as a private investigator. I've outed some pretty unsavory characters in my day."

The cop scratched his chin. "A P.I., huh?"

I nodded, and we said no more about that. "So did they just deliver the message and then let you go?" he asked after returning his attention to Mags.

"I think they planned to keep me longer, but something spooked them. Maybe the sound of sirens. I'm not sure, because it's all kind of a blur. They panicked and left. Once I was sure they weren't coming back, I got to work on the ties binding my hands. And once those were free, I took off the blindfold and made my way to the road."

"And that's where we found you," the officer concluded.

"Yes." Mags turned to me. "It's hard to believe that wasn't even half an hour ago."

"It's hard to believe a lot about today," Nan added.

Mr. Milton, who'd remained quiet until now, cleared his throat. "They took you to Dewdrop Springs. Probably means they're from there. A lot of the bad things that happen around the bay come from folks in that town."

All eyes zoomed to Mr. Milton. Nobody wanted to contradict him, but nobody jumped to agree with him either.

"It could have been anyone," I said at last. "But I doubt the kidnappers were stupid enough to return home while they had her."

"Are you saying we should rule out Dewdrop Springs?" Mr. Milton questioned, his voice flaring in irritation.

"No, but we shouldn't rule out all the other possibilities, either."

"Is there anything more you can tell us, Mags?" Mom asked, wrapping an arm around her niece's shoulder.

"That's all I know," Mags answered somberly.

I remained quiet. Mags had already been through so much. There was no point asking her to recall more when she'd already told us.

Did this mean the kidnappers wouldn't be found?

Probably at least not for now.

And who or what had scared them off? Would they really be back?

Would every moment going forward put me in peril, seeing as they could strike at any time?

They'd said they wanted me to stop, but I didn't know what I should stop. And honestly, I refused to be scared off my duties as a P.I. by some disgruntled bad guys.

More than afraid, I was angry—angry this had happened to Mags in my place, angry it had happened at all, and angry that Mr. Milton was still here.

Finally, I decided to say something about that niggling little problem. "Do you think we should limit any further discussions to family only?"

I looked to my parents for support, but it

was Nan who answered. "Are you trying to suggest Mr. Milton isn't welcome?"

"I just think it would be better," I said, "if it were only us."

When Nan didn't argue in his defense, Mr. Milton became extremely flustered. "I'm only trying to help. Can't you see that?" he demanded of me.

Mags spoke up in the eerie voice she'd affected since returning to us. "Angie's right. I want him to go."

Mr. Milton looked to Nan one last time, then stormed out of the station.

CHAPTER SEVENTEEN

"C'mon," the police officer told Mags. "We need to get your statement on record before letting you go."

"Should I come with you?" Charles offered.

Mags shook her head. "I didn't do anything wrong, so I don't need a lawyer present, but thank you."

We watched her go, the rest of us remaining in the waiting room uncomfortably close to a grimy looking coffeemaker. I hung back as far as I could from the untrustworthy appliance.

If it was a coffeemaker that had first given me my ability to talk to animals, then another coffeemaker could just as easily take that power away, too. Definitely not something I was willing to risk.

"How are you feeling?" Charles asked, leaning one shoulder onto the wall beside me and sweeping his concerned eyes over me.

"I feel like a giant weight has been lifted from my chest," I said. "I know that's super cliché, but it's also like a part of me didn't even realize that I couldn't breathe until Mags was brought back safe, sound, and relatively unharmed."

"I know what you mean," Mom agreed and laced her fingers through my father's.

"I don't know if we'll be able to find the kidnappers based on the information we have, dear," Nan told me, concern etched across her aged features.

"It's not a big deal. Now that I know they're coming for me, I'll be ready," I promised.

"Maybe they only wanted to give you that warning and plan to leave it at that," my dad ventured. "Are you going to listen?"

"Of course not," Nan answered for me. "Angie hasn't done a single thing wrong."

I simpered at my parents. "She's right, you know. Now that we have Mags back, we need to focus on figuring out who killed the judges."

"What are you thinking?" Mom asked, curiosity flashing in her eyes.

"I'm thinking I'd like to talk to Mr. Gable again. He's the one who knew the most about the Holiday Spectacular. Both the festival itself and the committee who planned it."

"Don't forget he's the one who knows the most about the guests, too," Charles reminded me. "He took pictures of everyone who came through that main entrance."

"Yes, the camera!" I cried. "It's here at the police station. I never got a chance to finish looking through it."

"That officer didn't seem too keen on having us involved in his investigation," Dad grumbled. "Do you really think he'd share a key piece of evidence like that?"

Charles shook his head in response. "He might not want to, but I bet that officer Bouchard could convince him otherwise."

"Already on it." Mom held up her phone

as the call connected. A moment later, a wide smile stretched across her face.

"Yes, it's me, Laura Lee. We found Mags, which you probably already heard, so now we're available to help you find the killer from the ice sculpture garden."

I couldn't hear the officer's side of the conversation, but whatever he said didn't slow Mom down one bit.

"Of course, I know you're all working on it very hard," she said, bobbing her head, "but you know how talented my Angie is, and I think she might have already figured it all out besides."

I made a slicing motion across my neck, begging her not to exaggerate our position, but it was too late.

Mom smiled even wider. "Yes, yes, we just need to take another look at those photos from Mr. Gable's camera to confirm. Would you mind letting us take a look?"

She paused while Officer Bouchard said something on the other end of the line.

"Luckily, we just so happen to be at the Glendale police station already, so if you would give the word to your colleague here, I'm sure he'd be happy to share."

I watched Mom as she marched in the direction the officer and Mags had departed and knocked on the door to the interrogation room.

Definitely not standard procedure, but Mom had never worried much about that. She would go anywhere, do anything to pursue a hot story, and this was definitely the hottest of the holiday season.

"Oh, officer!" she called through the door. "I know you're in there. I have Officer Bouchard on the line, and he has a message for you."

I stood in shocked silence as the door flung open. The officer cursed softly, then told Mags he'd be back in a moment. Sure enough, less than three minutes later we had Mr. Gable's camera in hand and free rein to look through the photographs.

"What are you hoping to find?" Nan asked me as I flicked faster and faster, taking in all the smiling faces from that morning one by one.

"I'm not exactly sure, but I'd like to see if any of the shots send up warning flares."

Although I didn't say so, I was also trying to determine who the two suspicious characters the rabbit E.B. had noted might be.

I reached the end of the photo roll and then began to flip back through in the other direction. Faster, faster, still unsure of what I was hoping to find, but knowing I was so close.

"Do you think—" my father started, but Charles held up a hand to silence him. He recognized something in my face before I'd even managed to connect the dots in my brain.

I shuffled through the pictures again, finally realizing that one very specific person was missing. "Nan, when did you and Mr. Milton join up today?"

"Why, he found me a few minutes after we arrived while you and Mags were still getting that fancy cocoa. You remember. Don't you?"

I nodded. "So he arrived before us, then?"

"Yes, absolutely," Nan assured me.

I found our photo in the lineup. We were one of the first. Only about ten folks had arrived before us, and none of them were Mr. Milton. Could he be one of the people E.B. had identified as acting suspiciously?

I wished I could ask the bunny now, but she'd already told me all humans look the same and I knew she wouldn't be able to recognize a specific person if shown a picture —not that I even had one of those since our old pal Mr. Milton had evaded the camera.

"He's not here," I told Nan, handing over the camera.

"Oh dear, don't be ridiculous." She flipped through quickly, her voice trailing off. "He probably took another entrance. There were several to choose from."

"I have a bad feeling about this," Mom mumbled.

"If you hadn't sent him away, he'd be here to answer these accusations for himself," Nan said, but I could tell she now worried about his possible involvement as well.

"He is a member of the committee, too, you know. He could have helped with information, but you never gave him a chance."

This behavior from Nan was shocking. She'd always supported me, no matter what. So to see her defending Mr. Milton now sent a chill rushing right through me.

"Nan, what exactly is your relationship with Mr. Milton? I never met him before today, and he just seems a little possessive of you."

"Oh, don't be silly," Nan responded. "He's an old friend from years ago, and we simply reconnected now."

"Do you think he's capable of murder or kidnapping?" I asked.

"How could he have been the one to kidnap Mags when he was with us the whole time?" Nan asked with a slight quaver in her voice.

"Okay. Maybe not the kidnapping, but what about the murders? He arrived before us and the victims were already dead by then."

"He would never," she insisted and bit her lip, a telltale sign she didn't quite believe the words that had come out of her mouth.

"Don't worry, Nan. I'm not saying he did

it. But you are right about one thing. We need to talk to somebody on that committee."

"Should I ring Mr. Gable?" Mom offered.

"No," I said, pushing her arm down even as she had already begun to dial.

"Just like Mr. Milton attached himself to us all day, it's possible the guilty party could be lingering very close to Mr. Gable now, and I don't want to alert him that we're coming. Not until we have the chance to talk to Mr. Gable directly."

"Have you figured it out?" Charles asked, rubbing my shoulders as if I were a boxer about to go in for round two of the fight.

"Not yet, but I feel close. Mom, Dad, would you please stay here and wait for Mags? I need to go now while everything is still clicking in my brain."

"Of course, honey," Mom replied.

"But be careful and call us if you need anything. Got it?" Dad added.

Charles, Nan, and I rushed out of the station with the pets in tow just as quickly as we entered. "We'll take my car," Charles said, unlocking it remotely so that Nan and Paisley could slip into the backseat and Octo-Cat and I into the passenger side.

I took a quick moment to explain my theory to the others.

"There's definite merit to that," Charles agreed, turning the key in the ignition. "It makes sense. I just hope we're not playing our hand too soon."

"Everything will be just fine." Nan sounded more like her usual self now that Mr. Milton wasn't around.

"Are we going to catch the bad guys now?" Paisley asked with an excited whimper.

"Yes," Octo-Cat answered for me. "It's time to make the canary sing."

He licked his lips at the mention of the canary even though we weren't going to confront a snitch—we would go directly to the guilty party.

CHAPTER EIGHTEEN

We found Mr. Gable at the sleigh same as he'd been before.

"Welcome back," he called as Nan, Charles, the animals, and I approached on foot, having parked just around the corner.

"Have you been busy?" Charles asked with a friendly smile.

"Things are slowing down now. Far fewer visitors coming into town, but we still have a lot of ticked-off vendors who want to have a word with the person in charge before they head on home."

Charles shifted seamlessly into the role of ace attorney. "Was the festival insured?"

"Of course we were. And thankfully we

should have enough to cover all the fee reimbursements, but I still don't know what the future holds for us. Whether the festival is done for good or it will continue on in a different place." The weight of this uncertainty hung heavily over his shoulders. Mr. Gable appeared to fold into himself as he considered the options, both of which were far less than ideal.

"But the Holiday Spectacular has always been in Glendale." Nan also didn't want to accept that things would likely be changing, and I completely understood where she was coming from.

Traditions were special because you could rely on them being the same each year, and I hated to think that my favorite part of Christmas could be going away for good.

Mr. Gable frowned as he noted the dejected look on Nan's face. "It has been, but we were chosen to represent the entire Blueberry Bay region when things were first starting up. It could just as easily be moved to Dewdrop Springs or Misty Harbor."

"Well, it shouldn't be," Nan clucked, eliciting a smile from Mr. Gable for the first time since tragedy had struck earlier that day.

"Where's E.B.?" I asked. Might I find some time to talk with the rabbit in private about my suspicions?

"Burrowed deep in the hay to stay warm, that sweet girl."

Upon hearing this, Paisley raced over to the nativity and began to dig furiously.

I set Octo-Cat down on the seat of the sleigh, and he remained quiet, wanting to hear what would happen next just as much as I did. I still didn't know whether it would be Mr. Gable or E.B. to give me the final intel I needed, but either way, I knew we'd find the culprit soon.

"Can we gather the committee?" I asked him now.

"I suppose we could. Why? Have you figured out something that could help us?"

"I think I may have a lead," I responded with a poorly concealed smile. "But I'd really rather share with the entire committee if possible."

Mr. Gable regarded me wearily. "Most of

them are still around, but at least one is other-wise occupied."

"Oh?" Charles asked, stepping closer as his interest grew.

Nan also watched Mr. Gable with wide eyes and shivering shoulders. The day was becoming colder as more and more snow fell, and we were all more than ready to go home.

We were so close now, though. I could practically taste it.

"Yes." Mr. Gable rubbed his hands together and blew out an icy puff of air. "Officer Bouchard is wrapped up in the homicide investigation, so I don't think he'll be able to put that aside for an impromptu meeting."

"He was on the committee?" I asked. Why was I only just now learning this? "That's strange, because he didn't recognize Zelda when we first discovered the bodies. And wasn't it Fred who was the last-minute addition rather than Zelda?"

Mr. Gable nodded as he turned this over in his memory. "I suppose he wouldn't. You see, Officer Bouchard only came to the meet-ings that pertained directly to safety and security. It's possible he either didn't pay attention to the finer details of areas that didn't concern him or that he knew about Zelda but was unable to connect the face with the name."

I nodded along, still finding it strange— especially considering Officer Bouchard served as chief detective whenever Glendale needed someone to slip into the role.

"Was it the same for any of the other committee members as well?" I asked, knowing we were mere moments from a big revelation.

"Yes, we had a couple who only contributed to certain areas just like the good officer Bouchard. Most of us were involved in all the planning meetings, though."

Nan went to join Octo-Cat on the sleigh. I worried that the cold had seeped into her bones. Even though she was in better shape than me, she was also quite old, and we'd been outside for much of the day in this frigid weather.

Charles whipped out his phone and opened the notes app. "Would you be able to give us a list of your members to help me figure out which were only partially involved, like Officer Bouchard?"

I watched as Nan settled in with Octo-Cat on her lap, glad they would keep each other warm now.

When I turned back to the men, I asked, "Mr. Gable, could you please also tell us which of the full-time members missed that last meeting, the one where Fred was added as a second judge?"

"Oh, sure that's easy. Just a second. I'll help you there, son." Mr. Gable and Charles worked out the list while I checked on the animals.

Paisley had cuddled her small, mostly black body against E.B. in the hay and was grooming her cheeks. The bunny trembled—probably afraid for her life—but I knew Paisley would never harm. She just didn't have it in her.

Octo-Cat watched the snow fall from his place on Nan's lap, following individual flakes as they floated down from the sky.

"It really is a pretty day," he said. "All the snow makes the sun shine brighter. It would be nice to take a nap if it weren't so wet—or there weren't so many murders happening around town, too."

I simpered at him and stroked his back. He always had a way of bringing things into perspective, that cat of mine.

"Angie, we've got it," Charles called me back to his side.

"Here's the full list. As you see, there are fifteen committee members in all that served this year. The ones with the stars only involve themselves in specific areas of the planning." He pointed to the names *Officer Bouchard* and *Janice Delacroix.*

"The ones with the question mark were involved in full-scale planning but missed the final meeting." He then pointed to *Bill Randone* and *Harvey Milton* on his digital list.

"Milton!" I almost choked on the name. "Is that Nan's friend, Mr. Milton?"

"What?" Nan cried, hopping down from the sleigh and coming to join us, Octo-Cat still curled comfortably in her arms. "What bout Harvey?"

"He was on the committee, but he missed our last meeting so he didn't know about the last-minute judging change up," Mr. Gable summarized. "And you know, Dorothy, I don't think I ever would have pictured you two as a couple. That Cupid works in mysterious ways."

"Can you tell us more about Janice and Bill? I don't know those two," I asked, shaking off the reference to my grandmother's love life, especially seeing as it concerned Harvey Milton.

Charles stared at his phone while Mr. Gable met my gaze. "Janice is our go-to marketing gal. She manages social media, the website, our newsletter. Doesn't really come to the meetings, but we send her everything by email. I don't know how carefully she reads over the materials we send her way, but she has access to the full information if she wants it."

"And Bill?" Charles mumbled, not bothering to glance up from his phone.

"Bill usually came with Harvey. They both had a long trek from Caraway Island, having to catch the ferry there and back."

Something tightened in my chest. "Caraway Island?" I asked as if I'd never heard of the place before.

Mr. Gable nodded. "Yes, and they both missed the last meeting due to something unplanned. I think Bill had to work late and Harvey didn't want to take the trip over on his own. Something like that."

"Nan, did you know Mr. Milton was on the committee?"

"Of course I knew," she responded, but her face crumpled a bit as I asked Mr. Gable my next question.

Now my heart began to gallop in my chest. We were so, so close. "Did you take a picture of Bill today?" I asked.

He thought about this. "Actually, no. I don't think I saw him at all until after we were shutting things down."

If I'd have been a cartoon, a giant light-bulb would have flashed over my head at this reveal. *Bill Randone,* that was the name of our guilty party. We had it. We had it at last. Now we just had to get him.

Somehow. Someway.

"Is he still here?" I asked, my words slur-ring together as I worked to get them out of my mouth as quickly as possible. "Is he helping to shut things down and send people over toward the park?"

"Last I knew, he was stationed over on Third Street."

"Let's go," I said, breaking into an immediate run.

Nan pulled right up at my side and matched my pace. At some point, she must have given Octo-Cat to Charles, because he ran a few paces behind carrying both the cat and the dog as he puffed along.

Mr. Gable hadn't joined us in the pursuit, probably because he didn't want to leave E.B. on her own.

"I just can't believe all of that," Nan said. "I trust Mr. Gable, but I also know Harvey didn't do this because he was with me the whole time. Do you think he knew about Bill?"

"There's a chance," I said between huffs. Running was still not a strong point for me, and somehow I'd managed to do it twice in one day now.

We ran another block before rounding the corner onto Third Street. And while I'd never seen Bill Randone a day in my life, I spotted him immediately because there he stood with Harvey Milton as the two carried on an animated discussion.

Suddenly they both glanced up and spotted us racing toward them. Randone immediately took off in the other direction at a sprint.

I grabbed my phone, still running, and dialed Officer Bouchard to let him know what we'd discovered and that his primary suspect was now on the run.

Nan pulled ahead, closing the rest of the distance to Mr. Milton faster than I could ever hope to move.

Then slapped him right across the face.

CHAPTER NINETEEN

I don't think I'd ever seen my Nan quite as angry as she was that day.

"You knew," she spat, her normally warm and friendly eyes saturated with a shocking coldness. "This whole time you knew and were probably even feeding information back to your friend."

Mr. Milton cleared his throat. Something I now realized he did whenever he felt nervous. "I didn't know for sure, but I suspected."

"Oh, you *suspected*," Nan repeated sarcastically. "So what were you doing just now? Warning him?"

"No!" Mr. Milton finally raised his voice to join in the fight. "I was confronting him with my suspicions."

"And giving him a chance to run." I jumped right into the fray as well. "Why wouldn't you have gone straight to the police?"

Picking up on our emotions, Paisley began to bark and growl and kick out her back legs like a chicken scratching at pebbles. "Bad man! Bad, bad man! No treats for you!"

Charles and Octo-Cat watched silently as the three women—two human and one dog —ganged up on a very guilty looking Harvey Milton.

"I don't agree with what he did, but I do agree with why he did it." This statement drew gasps from all of us, even Charles and Octo-Cat, who had chosen to mostly stay out of the confrontation.

"What?" Nan and I exploded in unison.

Mr. Milton shook his head. This time he didn't clear his throat, clearly feeling conviction in the words he was about to speak. "Caraway Island needs the Holiday Spectacular far more than Glendale ever did. The whole thing is a tourism goldmine, and our city is struggling. Due to the isolation, few ever manage to venture over. Each year it gets worse. Businesses are closing, and our community is becoming more and more cut off from the rest of the area. We need something… A magic bullet, if you will."

He winced. "Okay, maybe not the best choice of words."

I laughed bitterly. "The fact that you would say such a thing—even accidentally—just goes to show what a horrible person you actually are. It's like you think it's okay that your friend killed two people to try to bring more money into your city."

"Of course it's not okay," Mr. Milton responded, his gaze narrowing at me, "but we tried everything else and nothing worked."

"Everything short of murder," Nan mumbled and crossed her arms over her chest defensively.

Mr. Milton continued, keeping his eyes fixed on me. "When the planning started up for this year, Bill and I pushed for moving the festival to Caraway Island, but Gable and the others were quick to shoot us down. Bill said that Glendale wouldn't have a snowball's chance in hell of keeping the festival once a well-respected outsider got murdered on their watch. Naturally, Caraway would come to the rescue and agree to host going forward."

"And Bill told you all of this after the fact, I'm assuming." I tapped my foot in irritation. "Was this before or after your friend killed two innocent people? Oh, and the cops are already after him by the way. I spoke to my good friend Officer Bouchard while my grandmother was busy beating you up."

I thought I heard Charles chuckle under his breath, but it was hard to tell over the sound of Paisley's harried barking.

"Obviously, it was *after*. I already told you I had nothing to do with the murders."

"What about Fred Hapley?" I asked. "You mentioned shooting a well-respected outsider. But Fred wasn't either of those things. I'm sure most people tried to avoid his insurance sales pitch whenever they saw him coming."

Mr. Milton cleared his throat several times but remained every bit as angry as he had before resorting to this maneuver. "What about Fred Hapley? He got in the way. That's all. Bill missed the last meeting, so he didn't know the guy would be there. Luckily, he had a gun on him in case the icicle failed to do its job with the woman. The icicle worked, but he still found a use for the gun, anyway."

"Luckily?" Nan and I cried once again in perfect sync.

Nan reared back and slapped him across the other cheek. "I can't believe I ever considered you a friend," she said with disgust.

"If that's all, I'll just be going on my way," Mr. Milton said with one last look toward Nan as a giant frown took over his face. "It's really too bad. I liked you, Dorothy. I thought we had started something special. I can see now your affections are fickle."

"I don't date criminals," she hissed through gritted teeth.

"Believe what you want. I don't have to answer you anyway."

"No, but you do have to answer to him," Charles countered, drawing all our attention to the officer approaching from behind. It was the same cop we had run across earlier, the one who had questioned Mags and insisted on remaining in full control at the station.

Several paces back, Dad followed.

"Where's Mags?" I asked when he stopped at my side.

"Your mother took her home and sent me to find out what was going on here."

We watched side-by-side as the out-of-town officer slapped a pair of cuffs on Harvey Milton. Whether or not he planned any of it, he'd still been an accomplice by keeping his neighbor's secret.

As happy as I was to see Milton carted away, something still wasn't right. "What about the other guy?"

"Yes, what about Bill Randone?" Nan demanded.

"Bouchard's got him," came the answer. "That's right, you'll see your buddy soon enough at the station."

Milton drew on his right to remain silent, leaving the rest of us gaping until the officer escorted him from our view.

"Well, that's one way to celebrate Christmas Eve," Nan remarked with a shrug as we all burst into relieved laughter.

"I think I prefer the more traditional methods of celebration." Charles wrapped his arms around me and kissed my forehead protectively.

Octo-Cat got squished in between us but didn't utter a single meow in protest. "I knew it the whole time," he said instead.

"You did, did you?" I asked with another chuckle.

"The cat always knows," he explained, winking up at me.

Seeing as it was Christmas, I decided to let that one go. "You did good," I told him, backing out of Charles's embrace so he could breathe easily once more.

"You, too, Paisley. Good dog." I bent down and picked her up, and after having accepted a few pets and kisses from me, she vaulted into Nan's arms, completely uncon-cerned for her own safety.

"Whoa there," Nan cried, praising the wriggling little ball of fur.

"I'm sorry about your new boyfriend," my dad offered with a frown.

"Me, too," she said. "Luckily we weren't quite to that point yet, though."

"Think you'll ever forgive him?" Charles asked.

"Heck no," my grandmother shouted, then hocked a giant loogie onto the snow, drawing shocked laughter from all of us.

"Even though he swears he wasn't involved in the murders, he still warned his friend rather than turning him in. As far as I'm concerned, that's just as bad. I'd never be able to trust him again. Not after that stunt."

"You know what? Forget about Mr. Milton," I said. "He's not important."

"Actually, I do owe him one thing." Nan glanced from the street toward the sky, then met my eyes head-on. "I hadn't quite realized how lonely I let myself become since your grandfather passed. Of course, I have you and Paisley and…"

"And enough friends to fill a football stadium," Dad pointed out with a smile.

"That, too," she admitted her smile matching his, "but it's not quite the same as having a partner."

Charles pulled me into his side as we beamed at Nan and the touching news she'd just shared with us.

"So you think you're ready to date again?" I asked, my heart swelling with excitement for her.

"I think I'm getting there," she said with a sly grin. "One step at a time."

CHAPTER TWENTY

We spent Christmas holed up at home. Mom, Dad, and Charles all joined us at different points in the day, but mostly it was just me, Nan, and Mags sitting around our enormous Christmas tree and sharing our favorite memories from the years we'd missed out on celebrating together.

Nan, of course, dressed Octo-Cat and Paisley in their homemade holiday sweaters but held her tongue when Mags decided to wear a floor-length khaki skirt with a mint green cardigan set.

I opted to remain in pajamas, because nothing beats the comfort of flannel after a long, hard day—and the one we'd had yesterday was certainly a doozy.

That was Christmas.

On the day after Christmas, Mags finally taught us how to make candles the traditional way. Although I always loved learning something new, I didn't foresee many more candle-making sessions in my future. The whole process of dipping seemed to take forever, and I had nowhere near the skill Mags did when it came to swirling colors and carving patterns.

She made it fun, though, dropping random facts in here and there and entertaining us with a carefully curated collection of jokes.

I'd wondered if she was feeding us some of the same lines she gave her students back home. I kind of hoped she had.

We continued to eat up every moment together, but as the days passed, I grew sad knowing our time was almost up. I wished my cousin didn't live so far away because she'd very quickly become the sister I never had—and, despite everything, she said she felt the same way about me, too.

"Next time we'll have to get Nan and Aunt Lydia together with us," she said with a laugh I didn't understand, having never met Lydia for myself.

"Once we put those two together, all we'll have to do is sit back and watch while laughing our butts off," she added with a guffaw.

A couple more days passed, bringing us to New Year's Eve. Mags would be on an early flight out of town the next day. The rates, she explained, were far too good to pass up in favor of sleeping in.

I, however, balked when I saw just how early her flight was scheduled. "Are you going to be able to stay up?" I asked, having waited for the ball to drop every year since my mom had first let me stay up at the age of six.

"Of course I'm going to stay up!" she said with a scandalized gasp. "I might not even go to bed at all."

I laughed, Octo-Cat groaned, and Paisley danced, not quite knowing why. All was as it should be in my little corner of the world.

The doorbell chimed, this time to the tune of *Feliz Navidad*—in honor of Paisley's

Mexican heritage, Nan had informed me, even though that little dog had never stepped foot out of Maine a single day in her life.

Nan rushed to the entryway, fluffing her hair as she went. Her normal hot pink attire had been retired for the evening in favor of a sparkly silver dress. She looked like an award show trophy, and I looked rather out of place in my polka dotted pants and Grumpy Cat T-shirt. The latter had been a gift from Mags who said she'd never known anyone who loves their cat quite the way I do.

"Come in, come in." Nan's voice carried throughout the lower floor. "So glad you could make it."

I heard her exchange European-style kisses on either side of her visitor's cheeks and a moment later they appeared. "Happy New Year!" Mr. Gable announced cheerfully, carrying E.B. in one arm and a large bag of take-out in the other.

"Happy New Year!" Mags and I wished him back.

"Something smells marvelous," my cat said, perking up from his nap. He sniffed the air and then a grin spread between his whiskered cheeks. "Could it be…?"

Mr. Gable handed E.B. to me and the food to Nan, then ran out to his car for a second load.

"Hello again, little bunny," I said, conscious of Mags's eyes on me.

"Hello," E.B. answered all the while wiggling, wiggling, wiggling that nose. Mr. Gable returned with a triangular-shaped litter box filled with hay and fresh produce. He took his rabbit back from me and set her on the ground near the area he had fashioned for her.

Paisley trotted over, head held high. "Hello again, dear E.B. Do you still want to talk about your feelings?"

Oh, that sweet Chihuahua, always willing to do whatever it took to make others happy.

"What feelings?" E.B. asked, taking a tentative hop toward a piece of lettuce while keeping one eye glued to her canine acquaintance.

"When we met you at the festival you said you were always afraid that others would hurt you. Let's explore those feelings, shall we?"

Paisley tilted her head to the side, both ears perked high as she waited for E.B. to share.

The lop-eared bunny nibbled on her veggies for a spell, then said, "No one's ever asked me about how I feel before. Are you sure you want to know?"

Paisley plopped her wagging butt onto the ground. "Oh yes. I want to know everything," she said, her eyes sparkling with kindness. "Let's start with your childhood. Were you a happy baby bunny or a sad baby bunny?"

I stifled a laugh and left those two on their own.

Octo-Cat had followed Nan into the kitchen and Mags, Mr. Gable, and I now moved to join them there.

"I didn't know what to bring for our little New Year's shindig," he explained with an infectious grin. "So I stopped by my favorite restaurant and picked us up something to nosh on."

The logo for the Little Dog Diner was emblazoned across the bag, and scents of shrimp, garlic bread and lobster rolls now mingled with those of the baked goods Nan had prepared earlier in the evening.

Nan pulled each item out of the bag and set it on the counter.

The moment the lobster rolls made an appearance, my cat jumped onto the counter and twirled in three tight circles. "It is! It is! It is!" he cried as he spun even still. "It's my favorite food! Oh, Happy New Year to you, good sir."

I stifled another laugh. Sometimes it was really hard not to react to the animals in front of others, especially as I remembered E.B. using *Merry Christmas* as a curse word when last we met.

"Wonderful, thank you so much for bringing it," Nan said, and I could've sworn I saw a slight blush rise to her cheek. "Little Dog Diner is a favorite of ours, too."

"I'll get the plates," Mags volunteered.

"And I'll pour the drinks," I chimed in.

Nan plated up a nice variety for each of us, and together we retreated to the formal dining room table. None of us were big drinkers, so we shared a bottle of celebratory cider instead.

And although I hadn't known Mr. Gable

and E.B. would join us, I was definitely happy they had.

"What should we toast to?" Mags asked, a sweet smile tilting her lips upward.

"Well, first of all, *to you*," I sang out. "To you being a part of this family. To us getting to know and love you. And to you surviving the kidnapping."

We all laughed at the not-so-distant memory.

"I'll drink to that," Mags said with a giggle.

"Wait. Just you wait one second," Nan clucked. "I want your resolutions. That's right, all of you."

Mr. Gable stood. "I resolve that this year no one will get injured on my watch."

"Does that mean the Holiday Spectacular is returning to Glendale?" I asked hopefully.

"Not quite," he answered with a small sigh. "We're moving it to Cooper's Cove, but the remaining committee members, those who haven't gone to jail, elected to keep me as the head. And I of course was happy to accept."

Cheers rose around the table.

"That's awesome!" Mags enthused. "But I hope you don't mind that I probably won't be going next year."

We all laughed again. My heart remained light, mostly because I knew I'd be seeing lots more of Mags in the months to follow. In fact, we'd already begun planning a family reunion for the coming summer.

"All right, who's next?" Nan asked, looking between Mags and me and waiting for one of us to volunteer resolutions.

"Mine's easy," I said, shooting to my feet and lifting my glass. "This will be the year I get my private investigation firm off the ground."

"*Our*," Octo-Cat corrected, though only I understood. "And when do I get my lobster roll?"

Mags drummed her fingers on the table-top. "I don't know what I want out of this year other than to try new things. New things are what brought us together, after all, and I don't think I've ever been happier than I am now."

"That's a bold proclamation given what

happened on Christmas Eve," Mr. Gable quipped.

"It is," she agreed, "but it also speaks of just how much I love my new cousin and my new Nan."

Nan and I both *awww*ed.

When the table grew quiet again, Nan rose with her drink in hand. "I live every day like it's my first, my last, my everything. That's how you make life fun, you know. But this year I'm going to be a bit more careful about who I let into my life, and maybe this year I'll even find love again."

She glanced coyly toward Mr. Gable, who blushed and looked away.

My heart did a giant happy somersault. I never would've pictured the two of them together but seeing it now made perfect sense. I wondered if they felt it, too. If they were already well on their way to something wonderful together.

Yes, the next year was looking pretty good as we dove into our meals, chatting and drinking happily enjoying the good company.

"Ahem," my cat said, jumping onto the

table and flicking his tail ominously. "Aren't you forgetting something?"

Ugh. I *had* forgotten his lobster roll in all the excitement over Nan and Mr. Gable's possible forthcoming relationship.

"Off the table," I told him, taking half of my lobster roll and setting it on the floor so that he would leave me in peace.

He jumped down after it, joy sparking in his amber eyes. He moved quickly but not quite enough.

As if from thin air, Paisley appeared and snatched the treat away, racing back toward E.B. with the giant hunk of food protruding from her impossibly small mouth.

"Unhand my sandwich, thief!" Octo-Cat cried.

"I'm sorry, Octavius," she said, blinking slowly, as she regarded him. "I've been looking forward to this ever since I first smelled these things at the festival. You didn't share then, but it's okay. I forgive you."

"Angela!" my cat cried, staring at me in horror. "She took my sandwich! She stole it!"

I laughed, unable to hide my amusement any longer.

I tossed him a large shrimp, which he pawed at morosely.

"It's not the same" he mewled.

No, it wasn't the same.

Nothing was the same as it had once been.

But you know what? Ever since Mags and Mr. Gable had joined our lives, *it was better.*

I couldn't wait to see what the next year would bring.

WHAT'S NEXT?

Nobody does the holidays like small-town Maine, and my particular small town just so happens to be the very best at decking the halls and rocking around the big Christmas tree downtown.

Yes, every year, Glendale puts on a Holiday Spectacular that's grander and greater than the one that came before. Unfortunately, the only thing everyone's going to remember this year is the two dead bodies that show up in the center of the ice sculpture garden.

With the whole town having come out to play, everyone's in close proximity to the crime scene—and everyone's a suspect. A great many fingers are pointed my way, too, since it was me and my cat that discovered the deathly duo. With only my whacky Nan, recently discovered cousin, overly optimistic Chihuahua, and snarky feline to help me, can I clear my name and save Christmas all in one perfectly executed investigation?

Hold on to your jingle bells, because it's going to be a wild ride.

Pre-order to save! RETRIEVER RANSOM is just $2.99 until it releases on January 15.

Get your copy here!
mollymysteries.com/RetrieverR

SNEAK PEEK: RETRIEVER RANSOM

My name is Angie Russo. I live in the Blueberry Bay region of Maine, and I can talk to
animals. Thanks to this unique—but mostly
secret—skill, I've taken to solving mysteries
around town.

Usually my involvement happens because
I have a tendency to wind up in the wrong
place at the wrong time, but now I've also
hung out my hat as a private investigator. And
just because I don't have any clients, that
doesn't mean I'm not good at what I do.

Or more accurately, that *we're* not good at
what we do.

Yeah, my cat is my business partner, and
we also get help from my quirky nan, her

sweet Chihuahua Paisley, my lawyer boyfriend Charles, and even the handful of animals that live near our property—most notably, Pringle the raccoon who lives in a luxury tree fort in our backyard and is a tad addicted to reality TV.

Nan and Charles can't talk to the animals like I do.

In fact, I've never met another living soul who can, and I still don't know why I was blessed with this particular ability. All I know is that I got zapped by a faulty coffee maker, knocked unconscious, and woke up with a talking cat on my chest.

At first, I could only understand that one cat, but over time, my powers grew stronger. Now I can understand most animals, but occasionally I do still find a dud.

That same crabby tabby, Octo-Cat, wound up with me after we worked together to solve the murder of his previous owner. He came with a generous trust fund, a large coastal manor, and an endless string of color commentary about my life.

He has a girlfriend, a former show Himalayan named Grizabella. Their relationship is long distance and mostly sustained through my Instagram account. It's equal parts adorable, hilarious, and groan-inducing.

But, hey, a happy cat means a happy me.

And I have a lot to be happy about lately, especially since my bad luck often results in good outcomes. First there was the zap that gave me Octo-Cat, then Nan's impulsiveness landed Paisley in our lives, but those are nothing compared to the fact that a huge family secret had recently been cracked wide open.

Mom and I found out that Nan hadn't been completely honest about our family's origins even though she'd had more than fifty years to come clean. And, well, as awful as that whole thing was to discover, it also meant we were able to connect with long-lost family in Georgia, and thus I found the sister I never had in my cousin Mags.

She came for a visit over the holidays and that went well…

Mostly.

She still doesn't know my secret, but I think I'll tell her next time we're together. I probably should have told her before she returned home, but I was scared it would make her and the rest of our newfound family reject me.

I mean, did you believe me at first when I said I could talk to animals?

It's totally crazy, but also totally true and totally a defining feature of my life—and I wouldn't have it any other way.

That brings us to today.

We just celebrated the start of a new year. Normally I don't make resolutions, but this time I decided to do whatever it takes to finally get Octo-Cat's and my P.I. business off the ground. Even though we can easily live off his trust fund and Nan's retirement, there's a special brand of shame in having to be supported by your cat.

I mean, I have seven associate degrees.

At least one of those should be good for a job.

And a job is exactly what I'll have to get if my business doesn't take off this year. My boyfriend Charles said he'd welcome me back at the law firm anytime, and while I love him dearly, I always hated being a paralegal.

It doesn't matter, though, because I will

succeed at this P.I. thing.

I'm too stubborn not to.

Besides, I'd really hate to let my cat down...

"This is so exciting," Nan trilled as we stood outside of City Hall with a small crowd of other Glendalians to watch the incoming mayor get sworn into office.

Paisley barked merrily from within my grandmother's arms.

Octo-Cat had requested to stay home, given his disdain for crowds, and that was a battle I hadn't wanted to fight.

The mayor appeared at the top of the steps dressed in a fine navy suit with a light blue dress shirt and matching tie. At forty-seven, he was at least two decades younger than his predecessor. But while Mayor McHenry had been a family man, incoming mayor Dennison was a proud bachelor.

When asked about his singlehood by the press, he always said that his trusty golden retriever was more than enough family for him. Besides, less of a home life made it easier for him to give his full attention to making the humble town of Glendale the best it could be. Good answer, right?

As Dennison moved toward the podium now, a harsh boo rose from the crowd. Nan and I spun and saw a line of protestors holding signs that called for the new mayor to be ousted before he'd even fully taken up office.

"That's in poor taste," Nan hissed, shaking her head.

"Why does everyone hate him so much?" I whispered.

She shrugged. "Any time the party in office changes, somebody's bound to be unhappy about it. The whole country's a powder keg, so why not our town, too?"

I returned my gaze to Dennison, who stood stock-still with an unreadable expression. Poor guy. He'd won the election fair and square, yet he couldn't even enjoy this pinnacle moment in his career.

"What's going on, Mommy?" Paisley asked, wagging her tail in excitement, misreading the mood of the crowd.

I kissed her on the head and whispered, "Don't worry about it."

As much as I loved the optimistic little dog, explaining everything to her all the time often became exhausting—especially when we were in public and I couldn't speak freely.

"People of Glendale," the new mayor's voice boomed despite the continuing sounds of protest. "Thank you for electing me to serve as your mayor."

The boos and calls for him to resign grew louder.

Nan whooped and cheered beside me even though I knew for a fact she hadn't voted for him. She smiled at me sheepishly. "Poor guy. Someone needs to encourage him."

Now we both cheered.

Dennison's eyes met mine, and he nodded subtly before continuing. "I promise to do everything in my power to make these next four years prosperous and safe for all of us. Thank you."

He dipped his head, then disappeared back inside the building.

Octo-Cat would definitely be upset at

having missed the drama of this day.

"Well, that was the shortest inauguration I've ever seen, and I've been to all of them since moving out here some forty years ago," Nan mused.

"I'm sure it will be fine," I mumbled. "People just need time to cool off after the election."

"Yes, because of all of November and December and most of January obviously weren't enough," Nan responded after sucking air through her teeth.

We stood in place waiting for the crowd to disperse. Some of them did, but the protestors seemed to grow in number as they crept closer to the stairs outside city hall.

"Let's get out of here," Nan said, shaking her head sadly.

I couldn't agree more.

Pre-order to save! RETRIEVER RANSOM is just $2.99 until it releases on January 15.

Get your copy here!
mollymysteries.com/RetrieverR

WHAT'S AFTER THAT?

It's kittens for Octo-Cat when an orphaned litter shows up at our doorstep. And although the needy litter may be cute, the deadly mystery they bring with them is anything but.

Charles has been hinting at a big surprise he's planned for our first Valentine's Day together, but the arrival of the kittens quickly changes everything. Now he's helping me figure out who put the babies on my porch and why their paws are covered in blood.

Meanwhile Octo-Cat is left to play babysitter to the unruly brood while we investigate, and he's none too happy about it.

Right, so all we have to do is keep the kittens safe, solve their mystery, find forever homes for them, and try to find a way to salvage Valentine's Day. That shouldn't be *too* impossible…

Pre-order to save! LAWLESS LITTER is just $2.99 until it releases on February 20.

Get your copy here!
mollymysteries.com/LawlessL

MORE FROM BLUEBERRY BAY

Welcome to Blueberry Bay, a scenic region of Maine peppered with quaint small towns and home to a shocking number of mysteries. If you loved this book, then make sure to check out its sister series from other talented Cozy Mystery authors...

Pet Whisperer P.I.
By Molly Fitz

Glendale is home to Blueberry Bay's first ever talking cat detective. Along with his ragtag gang of human and animal helpers, Octo-Cat is determined to save the day... so long as it doesn't interfere with his schedule. Start with

book one, *Kitty Confidential*, which is now available to buy or borrow!
Visit www.MollyMysteries.com for more.

Little Dog Diner
By Emmie Lyn

Misty Harbor boasts the best lobster rolls in all of Blueberry Bay. There's another thing that's always on the menu, too. Murder! Dani and her little terrier, Pip, have a knack for being in the wrong place at the wrong time... which often lands them smack in the middle of a fresh, new murder mystery and in the crosshairs of one cunning criminal after the next. Start with book one, *Mixing Up Murder*, which is now available to buy or borrow!
Visit www.EmmieLynBooks.com for more.

Shelf Indulgence
By S.E. Babin

Dewdrop Springs is home to Tattered Pages, a popular bookshop specializing in rare editions, a grumpy Persian cat named Poppy, and some of the most suspicious characters you'll ever meet. And poor Dakota Adair has just inherited it all. She'll need to make peace with her new cat and use all her book smarts to catch a killer or she might be the next to wind up dead in the stacks. Start with book one, *Hardback Homicide*, which is now available to buy or borrow! Visit www.SEbabin.com for more.

Haunted Housekeeping
By R.A. Muth

Cooper's Cove is home to Blueberry Bay's premier estate cleaning service. Tori and Hazel, the ill-fated proprietors of Bubbles and Troubles, are prepared to uncover a few skeletons. But when a real one turns up, they'll have to solve the mystery quickly if they're going to save their reputations--and their lives. Book one, *The Squeaky Clean Skeleton*, will be coming soon. Keep an eye on www.QuirkyCozy.com for more.

The Cursed Cat of Caraway
By F.M. Storm

Quiet, secluded, and most importantly, far away from his annoying magical family, Guy couldn't wait to start a new life on Caraway Island. Unfortunately, he hadn't counted on his four-year-old daughter coming into her own witchy powers early… or on her accidentally murdering one of the PTO moms. Oops! Book one, *The Kindergarten Coven,* will be coming soon. Keep an eye on www.QuirkyCozy.com for more.

MORE MAGS!

Mags McAllister enjoys her work as a candle-stick maker in the historic district of Larkhaven, Georgia—never asking for anything more from her simple life. Then, one day, a white cat with mismatched eyes shows up outside her shop and refuses to leave—not for rain, not for tourists, not for anything.

Mags reluctantly takes him home, only to find that his presence changes everything inside her echoing plantation-style home. Nothing looks changed, but whenever Shadow is near, she can hear voices and sounds that shouldn't be there. Even worse, the next time she enters

her family's candle shop, she meets a disem-
bodied voice who shares her name and claims
Mags will also share her fate if they can't
solve the mystery that's haunted this location
since 1781… and quickly, because she won't
be able to maintain her strength for long.

Talk about a cold case!

Can the twenty-first-century Mags finally free
her eighteenth-century counterpart, or has
Shadow just signed her death warrant by
opening her ears to the supernatural secrets
that surround her normally sleepy small
town?

**To be notified when SECRETS OF THE
SPECTER (the first in Mags's new
series) goes live, make sure you sign
up for Molly's newsletter at
mollymysteries.com/subscribe**

**You definitely don't want to miss what
happens next!**

ABOUT MOLLY FITZ

While USA Today bestselling author Molly Fitz can't technically talk to animals, she and her doggie best friend, Sky Princess, have deep and very animated conversations as they navigate their days. Add to that, five more dogs, a snarky feline, comedian husband, and diva daughter, and you can pretty much imagine how life looks at the Casa de Fitz.

Molly lives in a house on a high hill in the Michigan woods and occasionally ventures out for good food, great coffee, or to meet new animal friends.

Writing her quirky, cozy animal mysteries is pretty much a dream come true, but she also goes by the name Melissa Storm (also a USA Today bestselling author, yay!) and writes a very different kind of story.

Learn more, grab the free app, or sign up for her newsletter at www.MollyMysteries.com!

MORE FROM MOLLY

If you're ready to dive right in to more Pet Whisperer P.I., then you can even order the other books right now by clicking below:

Kitty Confidential

Terrier Transgressions

Hairless Harassment

Dog-Eared Delinquent

The Cat Caper

Chihuahua Conspiracy

Raccoon Racketeer

Himalayan Hazard

Hoppy Holiday Homicide

Retriever Ransom

**Lawless Litter**

**Legal Seagull**

**Scheming Sphynx**

**Deer Duplicity**

**Persian Penalty**

**Grizzly Grievance**

CONNECT WITH MOLLY

Sign up for Molly's newsletter for book updates and cat pics:
mollymysteries.com/subscribe

Download Molly's app for cool bonus content:
mollymysteries.com/app

Join Molly's reader group on Facebook to make new friends: **mollymysteries.com/group**

Made in the USA
Monee, IL
12 January 2021

57449893R00121